TENNESSEE

W9-ASI-054

PIGEON RIVER

COSBY
DAVENPORT GAP

NEWFOUND MOUNTAINS

CATALOOCHEE

JACO SHOO

OKY MOUNTAINS

BALSAM MOUNTAINS

SOCO GAP

RICHLAND CREEK

WAYNESVILLE

TUCKASEEGEE RIVER

QUALLATOWN

BALSAM GAP

NORTH CAROLINA

COWEE MOUNTAINS

BALSAM MOUNTAINS

SNOWBIRD MOUNTAINS

NANTAHALA RIVER

NANTAHALA MOUNTAINS

LITTLE TENNESSEE RIVER

FRANKLIN

THE BLUE RIDGE

VALLEY TOWN

VALLEY RIVER MOUNTAINS

PHY
FIRST CREEK

TUSQUITTEE MOUNTAINS

STANDING INDIAN

CHUNKY GAL MOUNTAIN

SHOOTING CREEK

HAYESVILLE

SSTOWN BALD

HIAWASSEE

CULLASAJA RIVER

RABUN GAP

CLAYTON

JACKET RAID: ▬ ▬

10 Miles

N

SOUTH CAROLINA

Hiwassee

Hiwassee
A Novel of the Civil War

Charles F. Price

Academy Chicago Publishers

Academy Chicago Publishers
363 W. Erie Street
Chicago, IL 60610

Library of Congress Cataloging-in-Publication Data

Price, Charles F., 1938–
    Hiwassee / Charles F. Price
        p.   cm.
        ISBN 0-89733-429-9
        1. North Carolina—History—Civil War, 1861–1865—Fiction.
    2. Farm life—North Carolina—Hiwassee River Valley—Fiction.
    3. Chickamauga (Ga.), Battle of, 1863—Fiction.   I. Title.
    PS3566.R445H59   1996
    813'.54—dc20   95-50688
                                                                    CIP

For My Mother
Who Always Believed

Acknowledgements

❂ ❂ ❂

A number of people helped directly or indirectly in the writing of this book, whom I wish to thank. First among them is my nephew, David C. Galloway of Burnsville, North Carolina, whose genealogical researches stimulated my interest in my Curtis and Price forebears. My sister, Wanda P. Galloway of Bald Creek, North Carolina, encouraged me to believe the project a worthy one whenever I doubted it, which was often.

I am indebted to Weymouth T. Jordan, Jr, of the North Carolina Division of Archives and History, editor of the mammoth series *North Carolina Troops, 1861–1865: A Roster*, for providing me copies of out-of-print material on the service record and roster of Company F, 65th North Carolina Cavalry Regiment.

Two books in particular were useful in helping me understand the war in the southern highland: William R. Trotter's *Bushwhackers: The Civil War in North Carolina: The Mountains* (John F. Blair, 1988) and *Storm in the Mountains: Thomas's Confederate Legion of Cherokee Indians and Mountaineers*, by

Vernon H. Crow (Press of the Museum of the Cherokee Indian, 1982).

Of course, any errors of fact or interpretation are entirely my own.

No one could write about North Carolina soldiers in the Civil War without consulting the regimental histories found in *North Carolina Regiments, 1861–1865*, edited by Walter Clark and originally published in four volumes by the State of North Carolina in 1901. A welcome facsimile reprint of this work was published in 1991 by the Broadfoot Publishing Company, Wilmington, North Carolina.

Finally, I am indebted beyond measure to Anita and Jordan Miller of Academy Chicago Publishers for believing in me and in the value of this work.

Book One: The Raid

Book Two: The Battle

Book Three: The Return

Maps

Front endsheets: The Route of the Yellow Jacket Raid

Back endsheets: The Chickamauga Battlefield

Book One

● ● ●

The Raid

Chapter One

❁ ❁ ❁

1

Near the end of August, Bridgeman the bushwhacker and fifty of his Yellow Jackets left Davenport Gap and turned up the valley of the Pigeon River along the old Indian war trail towards the blue wall of the mountains.

Although Bridgeman pretended to be a colonel in the regular service and claimed he carried orders given him by General Burnside up on the Cumberland, in fact he held no rank at all and the Yellow Jackets were nothing but a crowd of renegades. They said they were part of George Kirk's band of partisans, but since Kirk's people were themselves infamous robbers, this hardly improved their standing.

Bridgeman boasted that he meant to chastise the secesh in all the country back of the Nantahalas. The Government of the United States had yet to lay its hand on the damned rebels in Macon and Clay and Cherokee, he said, as if there was a way any man could tell the unionists from the disloyal in those tormented highlands where the fathers were divided against the sons, neighbors lay in ambuscade for one another, and deserters from both armies lurked at the head of every cove. The truth of the matter was that Bridgeman had been raised an orphan on Downings Creek at the foot of the Tusquittees and had had a thin time of it, and there were scores he wanted to settle in that region.

Ahead of them, as they followed the winding valley of the Pigeon, stood line on line of high tops with the fog lifting off them, and there was a veil of mist over the river that they climbed above and looked down on, that resembled a boll of cotton drawn out thin. The air smelled of pine and as they rode higher it cooled and blew the odor of the river into their faces. They camped the first night by the rapids in a grove of yellow birch with sheer cliffs towering over them that seeped water so fresh and cold it made the jaws ache to drink of it.

On the second day they rode single-file along a narrow track over the gorge, in and out of sun-glare and twilight as they ascended through the layers of cloud that were clinging to the crowns of the red spruce and walnut and oak. Swathes of warm rain would drench them, then presently the sun would come to burn the damp off them in coiling wisps of steam. Towards evening a thunderstorm moved out of the Smokies and they took shelter under granite overhangs where deer laurel grew in thickets and woodbine hung down in tendrils, and they held the heads of the horses while rainspouts roared off the rock faces around them and lightning crackled in the valley at their feet. The third day they moved up Cataloochee and into the open country around Richland Creek.

Ever since the old days when Bishop Asbury used to preach at Jacob Shook's, there had been a Methodist campground at that place, and it happened that a parson named Talley was holding a meeting there by the river behind Shook's old house, when Bridgeman and the Yellow Jackets came up the road from Iron Duff. Talley ventured out to meet them, clasping his testament to his breast. Behind him the timid faces of his flock bloomed like morning-glories around the jambs and windowsills of the camp buildings.

Prodding the Reverend with the snout of his Maynard carbine, Bridgeman arraigned him for a god-damned intractable rebel. "In fact," cried Bridgeman, "I'll warrant this whole assembly is nothing but a combination of dirty secesh, come together to plot injury to them as holds the Union dear."

Now it happened that Talley was a rebel indeed, having served till the previous March as chaplain to the 39th North Carolina State Troops, and had returned home only because of taking a fever and developing a weakness of the lungs that made him cough blood in wet weather. But he protested to Bridgeman that he personally took no part in the disagreement between the states. Let Bridgeman observe for himself, he pleaded, how the folk gathered here were nothing but innocent wives, grandmothers, widows, orphans, and exempted men, worshippers celebrating the boundless love of the Lord Jesus and anxious only to hear His Gospel powerfully exhorted.

One of the Yellow Jackets they called Liver and Lights dismounted and put a brass-frame revolver to Talley's ear and made him kneel and address a prayer to the horse that Bridgeman was riding. They collected the people and robbed them of what little hard money and valuables they had on them, insulting the womenfolk with vulgar talk. They told the nigras they might now count themselves free persons of color, thanks to Massa Lincoln's proclamation of last January, and when the bucks and old uncles lingered around with an air of uncertainty, they chased them off firing revolvers at their heels. Some of them took the best-looking wenches behind the tub mill and ravished them. They gathered all the mules and horses and set the camp buildings afire.

"I'm obliged to kill one of you rebels before I go," Bridgeman announced as the fires began to crackle. He instructed Talley to consult with his congregation and nominate the man. After considerable travail, they presented Bridgeman a half-wit named Wren. Wren lived in a shack up on Buckeye Cove and faithfully attended all the camp meetings and always sat on the last bench picking his nose and eating the boogers. He had a little white rat terrier that went everywhere with him. Liver and Lights sat Wren down by the millrace and shot him in the back of the head. After that, the rat terrier attached itself to Liver and Lights; it was trotting along behind him that afternoon when the Yellow Jackets took the turnpike west between the wooded hills towards the Great Balsams.

Bridgeman could have gone on through Soco Gap and around by the Qualla Boundary, but there were always companies of the Thomas Legion quartered on the reservation. It was only a year ago that a party of Thomas's Cherokees had killed and scalped some of General Morgan's Indiana boys up by Baptist Gap, and since then nobody who wore the blue wanted to tangle with those Qualla redskins. Bridgeman turned southwest. The column skirted Waynesville and rode up the long, high valley between soaring crests clad in Fraser fir towards the notch, and on the fourth day they passed over the divide and started down the twisting switchbacks with the crags of the Cowee range rising in front of them. That morning, some of the Home Guard from Haywood County—roused by the Reverend Talley at Shook's—crept up to the edge of the turnpike and fired on them from a stand of hemlocks, killing a man called Fly-Speck. A volley from the Yellow Jackets drove them off, and Bridgeman turned south, leaving Fly-Speck where he lay.

On the fifth day they were climbing under Rocky Face Knob in the Cowees through a great deadfall of pines. All the way from Shook's, Bridgeman had been sending squads of riders up the glens and hollows on either side of the turnpike to clean out the farmsteads, so by the time they approached Franklin they had a considerable drove of cattle, sheep, horses, and mules to go with the stock they'd taken at the campground. Some of them carried hams and live hens dangling from their saddles, one had a shoat across his pommel, another wore a poke bonnet he'd stolen, with the ties fluttering around his head.

The folk here had seen little enough of war. Till now the worst of the trouble had been confined west of the Nantahalas. Consequently the Yellow Jackets seemed a terrible visitation. Tidings of their march were spreading through the whole section and all the farms and settlements in their path were deserted, the livestock driven off, the valuables carried away, nothing remaining but the poor chestnut-log cabins and the hay shocked in the fields and the corn standing in ragged rows and the apples ripening in the orchards. They burned each place as they came to it. Near Savannah Baptist Church, one of their scouts reported that the Macon Home Guard had been called out and was camping in the square at Franklin. By now all the enlisted men had been conscripted into the regular service, so there was nobody left in the Guard but exempts and the civil officers—the sheriff, register of deeds, justices of the peace, and such. Even so, Bridgeman elected to bypass the place. They left the turnpike and forded the Cullasaja and the Little Tennessee and started into the Nantahalas.

On the morning of the sixth day they climbed up through forests of oak, pine, tulip-poplar, and basswood. Tangles of rhododendron entwined with dog hobble encroached on one side of the narrow road and on the other they could look down a sheer rocky drop into a space where buzzards wheeled lazily on the updrafts. Always the far sound of rapids was in their ears, and now and then, when the trail bent around a shoulder of the mountain, they could see a curl of white water far below, or a thread of falls. Blue jays screeched at them from the woods. Sometimes they heard the shrilling of a hawk.

They passed between Standing Indian and Rattlesnake Knob, crossed Winding Stair Gap, and on the seventh day made their way at last over Chunky Gal Mountain. They stopped awhile at the head of the last descent to gaze west into the valley of the Hiwassee, the place where Bridgeman had been reared and where he aimed to square up his accounts. They were on a little sloping shelf grown over with sugar maple and late-flowering larkspur and partridgeberry. They could see down nearly as far as the Valley River range and Hanging Dog before the pearly haze over the Snowbirds and the Unicois obscured the view. On their right hand, the round tops of the Tusquittees crowded in from the north, wearing wreaths of pale cloud. To the south, past the dwindling line of Chunky Gal, they glimpsed the sharp peak of Brasstown Bald down in Georgia.

It was here that Liver and Lights discovered that Wren's little rat terrier that had taken up with him at Shook's was lost. He searched everywhere for it, whistling and calling among the laurel thickets and azalea bushes, but all in vain. So intent was he on finding the dog, that Bridgeman was forced to brandish his pistol and command him to mount up when the time came to resume the march. He was inconsolable.

2

For most of his life Madison Curtis had been a fortunate man. Of course, as he had often reminded Andy, his oldest son, a man's luck was nothing less than the fruit of his own industry and gumption. Anybody who sat back and waited for good things to drop into his lap from the heavens, as Andy was inclined to do, was unworthy of the blessings of prosperity and nine times out of ten was bound to be disappointed in life. By contrast, hard work inevitably earned good fortune.

Madison had been fond of recounting for Andy's benefit the story of how he'd commenced in life with nothing but a single horse and saddle and a patch of stony ground on South Hominy Creek down in Buncombe County, the whole of it worth no more than three hundred dollars. It had pleased him to tell how he'd come west after the Cherokee Removal and taken up a hundred and fifty acres of Indian land on the Hiwassee. Lovingly he would describe how he'd parlayed that first holding into a plantation of well over five hundred acres, a great wedge of rich bottomland and hillside pasturage stretching from Downings Creek on the east, along the river nearly to the place where Tusquittee Creek came down out of the mountains. On that generous tract he'd herded cows and sheep and enjoyed plentiful yields of rye, corn, potatoes, and flax. But sons are impatient with the stories their fathers tell about their own virtue and accomplishment; Andy had soon grown weary of Madison's edifying tales. Then, with the coming of the war and all of its attendant woes, Madison no longer had any reason to relate them and Andy, who'd joined the army in November of '61 with his younger brother Jack, had learned there were larger annoyances than a father's tiresome homilies. The fact was, Madison Curtis's luck had gone bad, and it looked like no amount of work and gumption was going to change it good again.

On this mild September morning, as he stood on the upper level of the gallery of his house, looking down the swale towards the line of beech trees that marked the course of the river, not a head of stock could be seen grazing in his pastures and not a furrow of ground was under cultivation anywhere under his eye.

The cattle had been the first to go. The Quillens, the family of tories who lived over on Sweetwater, had raided the place the same week Andy and Jack enlisted at Hayesville, and had run off eighty head. Madison and his youngest boy Howell had rounded up the last twenty beeves and driven them up to the high meadows on Double Knob, but one by one they'd been stolen away from there over the two years since, by the deserters from both armies who were hiding in the mountains. The last of the herd had vanished just days ago. All that remained to him were his saddle mare, a plow-horse, and a span of mules, which he kept stabled in a sort of lean-to he'd built onto the back of the manse. Each night somebody—Madison himself or his oldest daughter Betty or Andy, poorly as he was, or Andy's wife Salina—would sit up in the back bedroom with a lamp burning and the old Tennessee rifle propped in a corner, in case the thieves grew bold enough to try and spirit away the beasts from under the very eaves of the house.

The Quillens had got most of the sheep too, and the ones they hadn't stolen, the Pucketts from up Fires Creek had rustled, the two times they'd come down to pillage along the river. Night-riders had burned his corn crop last year just when it was ready for harvest, and his grain when it was heading too, and shot most of the hogs. This spring, he hadn't even bothered planting. How could he? Every few days some party of tories or bushwhackers would come plundering through. His servants had run off after that first raid of the Quillens', and with Howell serving in Folk's Battalion of North Carolina Cavalry now, somewhere yonside of the Smokies, all three of the boys were gone the better part of the time, and there was no decent help to be hired anywhere. The most he'd done was plant a provision garden close by the house, to keep the family fed, him and his wife Sarah, Betty and her two boys, the girls and Salina and Jack's wife Mary and their two children, fifteen mouths altogether—sixteen, now that Andy was back. For meat, he kept a sow and a boar in a pen hidden away up on Peckerwood Branch behind Downings Creek, and there was bacon and salt beef and pork in the attic and plenty of deer in the woods round about. At least, he reflected, they weren't starving. Not yet, anyhow.

He counseled himself that he must be content; God had smiled on him for many years. Now it was the divine will to test the faith that had been so easy to sustain when times were good. He prayed that he would prove worthy, that he would find the strength to bear adversity. He glanced over the ragged hayfields and across the river towards Cherry Mountain and beyond that to the high crowns of the ranges yonder in Georgia, as lovely a sweep of country as might be found anywhere in creation. Unless they killed him, they could not spoil the beauty of the high valley he had chosen for his home. The day he first saw it, twenty-four years ago, standing on the shoulder of Chunky Gal with all of it stretched out before him glowing with an amethyst light, it was as if his soul had arisen and soared out of his body to touch the face of Jehovah. Ever since, he had believed it was a sacred place, that God dwelled here.

He believed that still, though it was a good deal harder now. He walked to the corner of the gallery and sadly regarded the heap of charred timbers that had once been the most commodious barn in all of Clay County. A pair of Confederate deserters had done that, when Madison and Andy refused them bed and board at gunpoint only three days ago; poor Andy had got home just the evening before, on sick furlough from the Army of Tennessee, so weak from the bloody flux he could hardly stand. It pained Madison to think how pale the boy had looked, leaning against the gallery railing, drenched with sweat, frail and trembling as a sapling leaf, facing down those outliers.

It pained him too, remembering how hard he and the boys and his carpenter Black Gamaliel had toiled raising up that barn, fashioning the doors in the shape of Gothic arches, building that row of louvered cupolas along the peak of the roof to ventilate the haymow. It had been a better barn than most of the dwellings this side of Newfound Gap, that was sure. Today it was nothing but a mound of ashes, all those months of care and labor reduced to a smoking ruin in minutes by the spite of a brace of godless brigands.

These melancholy reflections were disturbed by the sight of a sorrel horse and chaise turning sharply off the main road up above and rattling down the drive towards the manse at an alarming pace. Madison recognized the rig as belonging to his cousin Watson, Uncle Amos's third boy, the high sheriff of Clay County. Watson was a man of stolid disposition, so all this haste looked shocking and unseemly. His white hair blew awry and his wattles shook like a turkey-cock's as he drew rein in a shower of gravel at the foot of the front walk and hailed Madison with a wave of his hat.

"Cousin," he cried, "I've just had a courier from Shooting Creek, says there's a column of Yankee irregulars on its way down, fifty or sixty of 'em, come around by Waynesville and over Balsam Gap, burning out the whole country."

Fear fastened a grip on Madison's heart. If such unholy

bummers were to descend on this place, which without a
doubt they would, the plantation lying as it did smack across
the middle of the county, likely they'd finish the ugly work
the Quillens and the Pucketts and all the roving outliers had
begun, and leave not one stone on another nor one beam
unburnt. But the calamity Madison dreaded worst was that
they would discover Andy. If they did, they would lynch him
sure. Anxiously he leaned out over the railing. "Are you
mustering the Home Guard?"

Disconsolate, Watson wagged his head. "Ain't no Guard
left to muster as I know of. There's you and me, maybe a
dozen others, that ain't enrolled. Looks like hit's every man
for himself, this time."

Madison vented a dry laugh. "When ain't it been? Why
don't you send up to the Boundary for the Legion?"

"Already done hit. Dispatched a runner to Valleytown
first thing. But Lord knows if there's any of 'em up there.
Could be they're over on the Tennessee side."

"Seems like they always are, when you need 'em," Madison remarked. What he didn't say, because it wasn't necessary, was that in peaceful times, the Cherokee were always
underfoot—foraging, they called it; white folk called it steal-
ing. Then when the outliers descended to thieve and vandalize, the confounded savages were nowhere to be found. But
there was no denying the value of their reputation; the Yanks
were scared to death of them. Bringing a company of the
Legion down from Valleytown just might turn aside this
pack of scoundrels.

"I've got to go, Cousin," Watson said, turning the chaise
in the cul-de-sac. "I'm warning all that's in harm's way."

"How about Amos?"

"Daddy's in the church a-praying." Uncle Amos, a min-
ister of the Methodist Episcopal Church, had built his chapel

on a broad hill south of Hayesville with his own hands after coming over the line from old Union County, Georgia, some years back. He often said he wanted to be buried behind the pulpit. If he was still there praying when the guerrillas arrived, he might well get his wish.

"God keep him," Madison called as Watson plied his whip and rattled off up the drive. "And God keep you." Watson wigagged his hat once more, swerved onto the road at the top of the ridge, and vanished in a drift of dust.

Dolorously, Madison watched him out of sight. There were urgent things to be done, but not before he got nourishment of the spirit. The cascade of troubles he confronted had put him in need of Scripture. He went indoors and down the steps to his library and took up his big leather-bound Bible and opened it to the first chapter of the Book of Job. A small and wiry man of fifty-one years, he lifted the great book between his unusually large, powerful hands. He had never allowed wealth and station to soften him, he had kept the whipcord look he had been reduced to by those early years of struggle. The head he reverently bent towards the page wore a fringe of frosty hair; it was pale as marble above, but below a horizontal line that showed where his hatbrim always divided his dome of brow, it was nut-brown from the sun, a farmer's coloring. Eyes of china blue peered between lids that the years of sun-dazzle had narrowed to slits. He shifted his jaw, chewed one end of his white mustache. He read:

> And there came a messenger unto Job, and said,
> The oxen were plowing, and the asses
> feeding beside them:
> And the Sabeans fell upon them, and took them
> away; yea, they have slain the servants with
> the edge of the sword; and I only am
> escaped alone to tell thee.

While he was yet speaking, there came also
  another, and said,
The fire of God is fallen from heaven, and hath
  burned up the sheep, and the servants, and
  consumed them; and I only am escaped
  alone to tell thee.
While he was yet speaking, there came also another, and said,
The Chaldeans made out three bands, and fell
  upon the camels, and have carried them
  away, yea, and slain the servants with the
  edge of the sword; and I only am escaped
  alone to tell thee. . . .
Then Job arose, and rent his mantle, and shaved
  his head, and fell down upon the ground,
  and worshipped.
And said, Naked came I out of my mother's
  womb, and naked shall
I return thither: the Lord gave, and the Lord
  hath taken away; blessed be the name of the
  Lord.

3

The fellow in the chaise went by like a cyclone, snapping his
whip over the ears of a sorrel colt that was so lathered it
looked like somebody had soaped it. Oliver Price jumped out
of the road and called that man a name he shouldn't have.
Instantly he regretted it, but there seemed little enough he
could do any more to fend off the evil influences army life
was always directing at him; he reckoned if cussing was the
worst he could be tempted to, he might as well be content. At
least he hadn't become a drunkard or a gambler, or gone with
bad women, like some of them. But still, it was a disappointment to find himself swearing so, after two sweet months at
home, well away from all the wickedness of the regiment. He

stood on the shoulder of the pike watching the chaise bounding away over the ruts and said a little prayer asking forgiveness.

That old jasper was surely in a hurry. Oliver wished he could move as quick as that. He was going to be late reporting back to his outfit, which was making up in Alabama, to be attached to Bragg's army. Some of the tardiness was his own fault and some wasn't. It was true he dawdled getting his traps together, after the word came that he'd been exchanged. But then, you couldn't blame him for that fool of a messenger getting himself lost—how likely was it that a fellow would go astray between Clayton and Rabun Gap, a distance of a scant eight miles, straight down the Little Tennessee?

Nor could Oliver be fairly condemned for postponing his departure. It was hard to leave off cuddling and dandling little silky-haired Martha, his precious babe of only eight months, who came into the world while he was away in Mississippi with Pemberton's army. Or to part with his son Syl, three years old now, a blue-eyed, rough-and-tumble joy. Or to bid farewell to his dear wife Nancy, whose particular delights it might not be proper to contemplate but which he could not help contemplating nevertheless.

Nor had he wished to part with the spirit of his poor dead older brother, which he knew was lingering still around the home-place. Freddy had been taken by the Yankees at Vicksburg at the same time as Oliver, but had fallen sorely sick and lived just long enough to get home after they paroled him. Freddy and Oliver had not been all that close—how could they, amongst ten brothers and sisters all contending for attention?—yet they had shared a kind of understanding about the world. They both believed it a good place beset by the Devil and a few bad men who did the Devil's work, and whom the righteous must resist.

He stepped back into the road and twirling his hickory staff he resumed his tramping. He had been just four days coming, on foot the whole way, following Betty Creek up from Rabun Gap to its headwaters and then keeping to the Indian hunting trails along the top of the Blue Ridge divide till he struck the road coming over the Nantahalas from Franklin. To somebody who had already walked all the way from Perryville, Kentucky, to Enterprise, Mississippi, and from there to his home in northeast Georgia, it hadn't been that much of a job. Besides, he was mountain-bred and traveling the tops was in his bones.

He drank in the warm sunlight that bathed these rounded foothills cloaked in hardwood forest and the sloping fields between the hills. The ugly mark of war was on the place— trampled grazing pastures, burnt-out tobacco crops, uncut hayfields with their naked ricks standing forlorn, row on row of corn cut down to rot, the bleached bones of dead sheep. Still, there was fresh growth in the burnt spots and the rough timothy-clover was thriving. You could see it was a land that would yield an abundance when peace came. There was one thing more he meant to do before going on to Chattanooga, where he could catch the cars. He wanted to visit the Curtis place. He supposed if he could be blamed for anything that would make him late, it was this, so hare-brained did it seem. But ever since the summer of the year before, in camp with Reynolds's brigade near Bristol up in East Tennessee, when he'd first heard Andy and Jack Curtis talk about their grand plantation on the river and the fine country it set in, he had an awful hankering to see it for himself.

Oliver justified his whim by telling himself that it was just as quick to go to Chattanooga through Clay County and out by Murphy as it was to go by way of Atlanta or around over the Blue Ridge through Macedonia and down Brasstown

Creek. He didn't know if this was so, since he had never gone either way. But he thought it might be. And even if it wasn't, seeing a promising new place was worth a deal of delay. Any good piece of prime country deserved looking at when you were a cobbler who wanted to be a farmer but had not a rod of land of your own to plant. The way Andy and Jack told it, a grain crop would grow belly-deep on that Hiwassee bottomland and corn would stand ten foot high, and there was dense, tender grass on the upland meadows that would make for great fat cows and milk heavy with cream and butter bright as gold.

Oliver was an optimist. He not only believed the war would end one day, he also believed he would survive it. He believed this in spite of what had happened to Freddy and all the terrible things he had seen and lived through. When it did end, when he laid down his musket for good, Oliver meant to be a farmer. Consequently, taking the time to look over the country around the Curtis place was an investment in the future. If it cost him two or three days more, what did that matter? He wouldn't be the only soldier late coming in from furlough. They'd be happy he had come back at all, the way things were going in the Army of Tennessee.

Two pistol shots broke the stillness somewhere up the valley behind him, towards the foot of the last mountain, their echoes twice repeated among the low hills. He stopped and looked back up the Franklin road the way he'd come. A thread of white smoke was lifting above the trees about a mile back. While he watched, the sharp crack of a carbine reached him across the intervening distance, and its echo spoke two times also. Trouble, that was. The jasper in the chaise must've been running from it, or hurrying ahead to warn folks. It annoyed Oliver that the fellow hadn't bothered to stop and warn him too. But then, not everybody in this part of the world thought well of a soldier no matter what color he wore. And there was always a chance that the people making the trouble were wearing the gray just as Oliver was. The line of smoke thickened and turned dark.

Well, trouble was nothing new to Oliver Dixon Price. He'd been in trouble one way or another ever since enrolling in the infantry company he and the boys had proudly named the Gilmer Lions but the Confederate States Army later insisted on calling Company G, 39th Georgia Volunteers. He'd enrolled down in Ellijay in March of '62 to escape the Conscript Law he knew was coming and earn that fifty-dollar enlistment bounty. He had chased bushwhackers and Yank cavalry, and been chased by them, all up and down the district around Baptist and Cumberland Gaps; raided into Kentucky with Kirby Smith, fought for Pemberton against Sherman's and Grant's boys at Champion's Hill and Big Black River in Mississippi, been besieged at Vicksburg and captured and paroled. He'd been starved and sick, laid out on account of homesickness and then come back on account of duty, been skeddaddled and shot at and abused and mistreated in more ways than he could remember. A line of smoke and a little shooting in his rear weren't likely to stampede him now.

He delayed only long enough to check the loads in his Colt's navy revolver and fit five Eley Brothers' percussion caps on the nipples of the cylinder and let the hammer down on the empty chamber. It wasn't a private's weapon, that pistol; it was the kind of thing only an officer was privileged to carry. But it was legitimately his very own; he'd plucked it off a dead Yank captain who fell in the ditch in front of his section of the line at Vicksburg, and had managed to keep it after the surrender by taking it apart and hiding the pieces in his blanket roll and haversack, and he fancied it. He especially liked the fine engraving around the cylinder, which if you looked close showed a whole flock of tiny sailing ships wreathed in the smoke of a miniature sea-battle. He stuck the Colt's in the top of his trousers and started on his way once more.

Presently he came to the big Spanish oak that the Curtis boys had told him to look out for, with its roots tangled in the bed of the road and its top shattered by lightning. Just as they said, a path split off to the left between a wooded hill and a broad piece of bottom. They told him the bottom was planted in tobacco but now it was burnt-over stubble covered with a new growth of weeds. A little branch ran through the bottom that had to be Downings Creek, the eastern boundary of the Curtis plantation. Whatever the trouble was, it looked like the Curtises were going to be spang in the way of it. That knowledge put him in a more urgent frame of mind. He took the turnoff and picked up his pace.

A short distance in front, the way around to the Curtises veered off to the right, and in the southwest corner of that fork there was a tumble-down farmhouse. The jasper in the chaise had warned the ones who lived there, and as Oliver approached, they were loading up an old sun-whitened wagon as fast as they could go, a man with a grizzled beard and his woman and a flock of younguns. The mules in the traces were turning their heads this way and that with their long ears up, watching those folks running back and forth, as if the sight amazed them.

The people paused long enough to give him the fisheye in case he meant them mischief, and he set off along the west fork towards the Curtis place. Then he heard the horses coming down the road behind him. Glancing back he saw the head of a mounted column, men riding two abreast, bending into the turnoff. At once he left the road and slid into the weedy ditch and then into a stand of cane growing beside the creek, where he hid himself. No sooner had he settled into the cane than he heard the wagon roll out of the yard of the farmstead; it went jouncing by, above him on the road, headed off west in the direction of the Curtis's, with the kids all a-wailing and the old farmer mightily exhorting those mules. Somebody on the turnpike fired a pistol at them and there was a gale of laughter. Oliver held his Colt's against his face with both hands, feeling the cool of the blued metal slowly turn warm against his cheek. He backed up in that cane like a turtle going into its shell. A lot of horses were coming towards him; he heard the jingle of bit-chains and the clang of sabre-scabbards and the thunk of canteens full of water.

Some of them stopped at the farmstead, but the biggest party went on towards the Curtis place above where he lay quietly in the canebrake. Between the shafts of cane he saw them go past. They rode every kind of horse and mule and wore every sort of clothes, hickory, rusty blue, butternut, gray, jeans, linsey-woolsey. Slouch hats and fatigue caps and one jasper with a poke bonnet on his head for a joke. No colors cased or uncased. Not a regular officer to be seen, though one of the jaspers at the head of the column had shoulder straps stitched to the yellow blouse he wore. Each of them carried a number of revolvers, stuck in sashes, boot-tops, pommel holsters. They smelled like old sweat and grime. At the end of the column there was a big drove of livestock.

Oliver dared not move even after they disappeared around the bend, for he could hear the ones who had stopped off at the farmhouse ransacking it. He listened to them breaking up the crockery and the mirrors and punching out the window-lights of the cabin. They cussed something fearful and one of them was giggling like a girl, on and on and on. Then after a spell the odor of coal oil came to him, and presently the smell of fire, and awhile later they rode away at a gallop after the others, scattering pebbles down on him from the road. He counted to a hundred before he got up out of the canebrake and climbed to the road.

He stood in the road watching the farmhouse burn. Sometimes, despite his natural optimism, the cruelty of the war filled him with despair. This was one of those times. So much was being lost. So many homes like this one, with all their precious memories. So many fine young men. He thought again of Freddy, dead of the wasting fever he'd taken in the muddy trenches south of Vicksburg. Freddy could make a little doll out of corn shucks that looked like it was ready to walk and talk. There'd been a twinkle of mischief he'd get in his eye when he took a notion to tell one of his funny tales. He could plow a furrow so straight it looked plumb-lined. No one could measure what was lost when a man died before his time—the dreams he'd never dream, the children he'd never get, the house he'd never build, the work he'd never do.

Oliver watched the roof-shakes shrivel in the fire, lift up in the currents of hot air and float away as wisps of ash. He saw the cracks opening up the stick-and-clay chimney in zigzag lines and catching alight. Presently the pin-oak roof caved in with a crash and a great rush of sparks, and the logs of the near wall collapsed, revealing the stone fireplace on the opposite side with the cooking-pot still hanging in it, red-hot at the heart of the fire.

Chapter Two

❖ ❖ ❖

S he bent over him while he slept and watched him shiver under the mounded quilts. He looked so frail that the thought of having to awaken him dismayed her.

It was Sarah Curtis's secret that, of the nine children she had brought into the world, her oldest boy was closest to her heart. She could not say exactly why. Betty was quicker, Jack was more able, even Howell seemed wiser despite his youth. All the others—her stairstep daughters Martha, Sarah, Polly, Julia, and Rebecca—had in them some of the fire that burned so pure and steady in their father. But the fire was out in Andy. It always had been.

She thought maybe that was the reason for her affinity. Where he was needful, the others were bumptiously self-reliant. Sarah had never been called on to bolster their spirits, only to answer the normal run of material need; morally they had flourished like honeysuckle. But Andy's soul always had to be tended, like some exotic plant that could be endangered by every change of weather. Maybe tending his wants had fulfilled some deep longing of hers. The strength that Madison and the other children had, they felt no need of sharing, while Sarah's substance always wished to flow out of her and bear up a weaker spirit.

Now, with the partisans coming, Andy was in special danger. She dreaded awakening him, seeing the fear rouse in him. He was altogether too delicate for the times they were in; the rough ways of army life were breaking him down. Last winter he caught the chicken pox and took a sick furlough, but after getting well he laid out for weeks because he couldn't countenance going back. That was before the bush-whacking in these parts had got so bad. Now, six months later, ailing in soul and body both, he was home again. But this time he was learning to his dread that it was hardly safer for him here than at the front.

Sarah Curtis, gazing with love on her son, was a forty-seven-year old woman whom toil and eighteen years of child bearing had made old before her time. She was scarcely five feet tall, but sinewy like her husband and nearly as strong. Her silver hair was parted in the middle and drawn tight to a bun fixed with horn combs. She had expressive brown eyes and a clamped mouth that looked parsimonious but wasn't.

As she stood pondering, Salina entered the room and, circling the foot of the bed, saw the worry in her face and demanded in her brisk manner, "What is it, Mother Curtis?"

Sarah saw from the settled way Salina looked at her that she could sense the peril descending on them, but did not intend to let it frighten her. Salina possessed all the power that Andy lacked, and God be thanked, she loved him enough not to resent it. Sarah rested a hand on her shoulder. "There are bushwhackers on the way. We must wake Andy and hide him."

There was not the slightest sign of perturbation. Confidently Salina nodded. "I'll fetch his clothes."

"He'll need some extra." Sarah opened the wardrobe.

"Father Curtis says hide him in the springhouse. It'll be cold there, and his chill will worsen." She leaned over him and touched his clammy brow, smoothed his damp curls with her finger ends. The sour smell of his sick-sweats rose powerfully. She spoke his name.

The blue eyes opened and focused on her—Madison's blue eyes. He shuddered. "Mama?"

"I'm sorry to bother you, son. But we've got to move you."

With pain she watched the alarm take him. "What's the trouble, Mama?" She told him, and was pleased to see that, except for shaking somewhat harder, he seemed to bear the news pretty well. "Give me the Harpers Ferry pistol," he implored.

"Your father says take the Tennessee rifle and the shotgun too. He's loading and priming them for you."

He protested, "That's every firearm in the house."

She shook her head. "We won't need any weapons. The ruffians will only want to rob us, and we've grown used to that. You're the only one that's in danger." It wasn't so, of course. If the raiders thought they were secesh, they might kill Madison or torture him, or both. But she was hoping Andy wouldn't guess that.

Salina came to the bedside carrying an armload of clothing. "I'll go down to the springhouse and stay with you," she told Andy, knowing it would comfort him. They never violated white women, or hadn't yet. But they often outraged them with ugly talk and sometimes even hurt them, and she knew Andy would be easier in his hideaway knowing she was safe from such slurs and dangers.

They dressed him in his pleated butternut blouse with the blue chevrons on the sleeves, and a pair of homespun pants. Salina tied the laces of his brogans while Sarah wrapped him in a woolen cloak and a knitted shawl. Betty's two boys, Jimmy and Andy, wearing identical outfits as always and looking like twins although they weren't, watched from the doorway, each with his arms crossed in precisely the same way. Bill Cartman, Betty's husband, enjoyed encouraging their imitation of each other, though Betty herself found it peculiar and, with Bill gone in the mountains to escape the conscript officers, had been trying in vain to break the habit. Between the pair of matched brothers, Jack's two-year-old son Alec stood blinking in fascination as Sarah and Salina put their arms around Andy and raised him tottering to his feet. Then the Cartman boys thundered off down the hallway shrieking with excitement and Alec went toddling after them.

For a moment Andy resisted. "If there's harm done you, I'll be too far away to help," he reminded them.

Sarah repeated, "There'll be no harm."

"Even if there is," Salina sensibly pointed out, "your being here would only make it worse."

Madison appeared in the doorway, stern-faced and gaunt, the Harpers Ferry pistol stuck in his waistband, rifle in one hand and shotgun in the other. About his neck he had draped a cartridge box and cap pouch on a heavy belt and a tin powder flask. Wordlessly he handed a long weapon to each of the women, then took Andy in charge and the four of them moved down the hallway to the stairs and descended slowly to the ground floor while all the children gathered around the upper landing to watch silently between the railing-posts. Eighteen-year-old Martha waited by the front door with her newborn daughter Eva in her arms. Sanders Barter, her husband, was off in the hills with Bill Cartman. As Madison approached the door supporting Andy, she ran to her brother and kissed him, bursting into tears. "There now, Sis," Andy soothed her with a valiant smile, "ain't a thing in the world to be crying about."

Standing by, carrying the heavy rifle across her bosom cradled in her arms, Sarah was as moved by Martha's pity as she was by Andy's show of courage. Since the war there had been a distance between them. Andy had gone for a soldier despite his fear and Sanders had laid out; Andy resented this and Martha hated how he sat in judgment on Sanders, who was a mild soul and anyway believed in union. But if the war could divide, it could also unite. With raiders bearing down, the family was closing ranks. Sarah wept for joy and dread as Madison and Andy shuffled out the door into the sun-glare and the children came yelling down the stairs behind her like an avalanche and they all moved out onto the gallery and for the first time heard the gunfire in the near distance, pop pop pop pop, and saw in the air the white ash whirling like snowflakes from whatever was burning that they could smell now on the wind.

Betty, her oldest child, came and took the rifle out of Sarah's arms, fixing her with a level, collected gaze. "I'll tote this down to the springhouse, Mama." Betty was secesh, no matter what Bill Cartman professed, if he professed anything. Nobody knew if Bill was a tory or just a coward, but they all understood about Betty and were wiser than to blame her for what her husband did or didn't do. One fellow had done that a year ago on the square in Hayesville, and she had horsewhipped him. Sarah watched after her as she descended the front steps with the rifle crosswise in front of her and her copycat boys Jimmy and Andy following along behind in step together, each with his arms swinging in time. Bill Cartman's Newfoundland dog came romping down the drive and as they started towards the springhouse it began running big circles around them, its tongue happily flailing.

Resolutely Sarah dried her tears and turned to address Jack's Alec and the three youngest girls, who were dashing boisterously up and down the gallery. "You younguns listen to me now. I don't mean to scare you, but some rangers are coming this way." The burnt barn, the tory raids in the night, the tales of shootings and hangings on nearby farms, all instantly came to mind. They stood still and gave her their earnest attention, wartime youngsters for whom play and danger had come to be interchangeable.

"We're a-hiding Brother Andy," Sarah went on, "because if the rangers catch him, they'll kill him." It was no use mincing words. The girls were all old enough to understand. Only Alec was too young. Gently she grasped him by the shoulders and called Mary over and told her to hold him close and keep him quiet. Lord only knew what he might say if the bushwhackers inquired of him. "Stay inside the house," she instructed the girls. "If they come indoors and say aught to you, nobody's to speak. Father Curtis and me will speak what words are needful." She drew a breath and demanded, "Now if there's shooting, or any kind of trouble, tell me what you're to do."

Without hesitation eight-year-old Rebecca spoke up: "Run to our secret places and stay till Papa comes."

Sarah took another breath. "And what are you to do if he don't come?"

"Wait till dark," Polly replied at once. "Then cross the river on the swinging bridge and go to town."

"Where in town?"

"Mister Watson Curtis's house," answered Julia.

Sarah nodded. "That's good." Martha and Mary stood by the front door with their infants cradled in their arms, and Alec, feeling the tension around him, had ahold of Mary's hoops with both arms. Sarah was displeased to see that

Martha was still weeping. It was all well and good to be concerned for Andy, but the time had come to stand firm. Sharply she advised the girl to control herself, and it was Sarah's namesake, her sixteen-year-old, who went to Martha and held the baby while Martha blew her nose and took herself in hand.

There was more shooting in the direction of Downings Creek and it was closer now. Ashes fell in a drizzle and the light faded and when they looked up they saw that a pall of smoke had dimmed the sun to a red disc. The odor of fire stung their eyes. Sarah turned around in time to see Madison and Andy, yonder at the end of the sloping meadow, descend out of sight into the ravine that led to the springhouse, with Salina and Betty on either side carrying the guns and the Newfoundland dog circling them and the two Cartman boys marching back and forth behind them in the uncut timothy, looking exactly the same, like little soldiers on parade.

Chapter Three

❖ ❖ ❖

Bridgeman raised his hand and brought the column to a halt in the narrow road. Below him to the left, standing nobly as he had remembered it on the nose of a hill, looking down a grassy swale to the river, was the white frame plantation house at the end of its graveled lane, the tin sheathing of its hipped roof glaring in the sun, rock chimneys towering at either end, the double galleries wrapped cozily around it. Rows of boxwoods led up to it from the turnaround at the end of the lane. A pair of big magnolias flanked the entrance and there were oaks and maples standing all about. A snake-rail fence bounded it.

In nine years Bridgeman had not forgotten that house. The finest place in the county, Ryder used to call it, pinching his mouth in envy. Nor had Bridgeman forgotten the man who lived there, old High-and-Mighty Judge Curtis. In Bridgeman's memory Old Man Curtis was a small but royal-seeming man, bone-gaunt, wearing a silver mustache, driving past Ryder's in a black calash with isinglass lights, drawn by a roan mare. Ryder used to swear at Curtis under his breath as the old man passed by, and would follow him with his muddy eyes. Ryder's belly was sour with a smallholder's hate for his betters. Bridgeman remembered Old Man Curtis had large hands ropy with veins. His nigra always rode along behind him on a fine saddle mule. He owned the kind of house a man would own whose nigra rode a saddle mule.

"By God," cried Porcupine, "think of the blaze that old place'll make." Eager laughter gusted along the column, but Liver and Lights loudly reminded them they must rob it before they could burn it. "Hell," Bloody Bob disputed him, "this whole damn section is plumb robbed out." It was true, Bridgeman glumly reflected. Everything west of the Nanta-halas had been stolen off or burnt out by bounty-jumpers and deserters, or tories and secesh raiding one another. When he planned this march he hadn't realized the hard case this valley was in. Up to the time they crossed the Little Tennes-see, the boys had enjoyed good pickings and had been gay. But lean times would turn them surly. Bridgeman didn't want that.

"I know this old man," he said. "If he has aught to rob, why, we'll rob him. But I mean to offer him a choice the way I done that parson over at Shook's."

"How so?" Porcupine wanted to know.

"This is a man sets great store by his god-damn virtue. I mean to test him in his righteousness. I'll tell him we won't burn him out if he'll give up the secesh he knows here-abouts and say where their goods is all hid." For he knew what goods remained had been secreted away and he would never find them without help. And it pleased him to tempt godly men by posing them ungodly choices. Making that preacher hand over the half-wit to be shot had tickled him plenty. It showed what hypocrites these holy folk were at heart: they'd betray a fellow in a minute to save what they held dear.

Bloody Bob scowled. "Whyn't we just burn him and to hell with it?"

"No, the Colonel's right," Porcupine spoke up. "This way, maybe we'll lay hands on riches we'd never locate on our own."

"And find us some real secesh to hang," Liver and Lights brightly reminded them.

"Shit," Bloody Bob said, "I don't care who I hang, union or secesh."

Ordinarily Bridgeman didn't either. But the fact was, he remembered Old Man Curtis in a right good light and preferred not to hang him or burn him out or do much more than just demean him. It was Ryder and his kind that Bridgeman despised. "Well, hell," cried Bloody Bob, "whatever deal he makes, let's burn him out afterwards." Bridgeman chose not to argue. He spoke to his mount and led them down the graveled lane. They passed a mound of charred ruins that looked like it might once have been a barn. Back of this stood three log slave cabins with weeds growing up through the holes in the porch floors. They rode through the open gate in the worm fence and some of them broke off and circled the house, and when those came whooping around the other side, they had with them a chestnut mare and an old white plow-nag and a pair of mules they'd found stabled in a lean-to fixed to the back.

Old Man Curtis came out wearing his frock coat and cravat and stovepipe hat, Sunday-go-to-meeting. He didn't look a day older to Bridgeman. He stood there on the gallery with his thumbs hooked in the pockets of his waistcoat and looked them over. "The question of the day," Bridgeman told him, "is whether you are secesh."

"'T'won't fend off ruin if I am or ain't," the old man stoutly replied. That brought a knowing guffaw from the

Yellow Jackets. Some of them got down and started up the walk between the boxwoods. A woman as bony and white-headed as Old Man Curtis himself came out of the house and stood behind him in a gingham dress and a white apron, with a fringed shawl thrown around her that was the color of mustard. At the sight of her, the ones that were coming up the walk stopped. Porcupine was one of them. "Have you got any darkey women?" he demanded. "I favor darkey women, I surely do."

Neither of them answered him or even paid him any mind. The old man looked at Bridgeman with pale blue eyes and the woman scornfully watched the fellows that had stolen their mules and horses. "We mightn't ruin you if you tell us the truth," Bridgeman said. "Are you secesh or not?"

"I'm union," the old man insisted.

Bridgeman dismounted and came up the walk, pushing Porcupine and the others out of his way. His sabre scabbard clanked around his heels as he went. He climbed the steps to the gallery and stood looking down on the old man, smelling his stale scent. Curtis gazed back unafraid. Bridgeman turned his head aside and spat tobacco juice into the crape myrtle. "I know you, Squire Curtis," he said. "I wonder if you recollect me."

Curtis examined him. "Can't say as I do."

"'T'ain't likely you would, I reckon. I was an orphan boy that Frank Ryder taken up. He raised me yonder on Downings Creek, till I run off nine years ago this very month, a lad of fourteen, weary of that old bastard's razor strop and assortment of hickory switches. Worked me like a very nigra, Ryder did."

The Old Man blinked once but that was all. "I calculate it was nine years ago they found Frank Ryder dead, chopped in the head with a hoe."

Bridgeman nodded with a smile. "Proud to say I done 'er. That deed made a man of me."

"Ryder was harsh, all right," Curtis admitted. "But he deserved better than that."

Expansively Bridgeman chuckled. "We'll disagree on that'un, Judge." Porcupine renewed his plea for a darkey woman and at last the old man took notice of him and with some exasperation explained that all his servants had run off months before. "Gone to freedom," he said.

"Yes," cried Bridgeman in triumph, "you're a slaveholder, and that makes you goddamn secesh. You've lied to us after all."

Bristling, Old Man Curtis rounded on him. "A man can own slaves and love union too," he declared. "Many in this country did, before the likes of you turned them against the government with your bumming and plundering." Bridgeman observed him indulgently. It was still vivid in his memory, even after eleven years, how Old Man Curtis had climbed down out of his calash on the bridge at Murphy and seized Ryder's arm while Ryder was larruping him with the buckle-end of a belt, fetching blood with every lick. It was market day, and the boy that Bridgeman was on that long-ago morning had dropped and burst open one of Ryder's watermelons, trying to rearrange the load in their old two-wheeled donkey cart after the uneven bridge timbers had disturbed it. Holding on to Ryder's arm, Old Man Curtis said, You want to beat something, beat that donkey. But leave off beating this child. Ryder stood six foot high and weighed near two hundred pounds. Next to him, skinny little Old Man Curtis looked like a child himself, except for his pewter-colored mustache and those wintry blue eyes and that big hand of his wrapped around Ryder's wrist. His nigra sat his mule serenely looking on. For just an instant Ryder thought of disputing Curtis, then his craven heart turned sick and he hung his head and murmured an apology. Old Man Curtis nodded, returned to his calash, and drove away grand as a nabob, with his nigra trotting along behind.

That evening, of course, Ryder flogged Bridgeman something awful, venting on him the hate he'd dared not show to Curtis. But Bridgeman had been grateful nevertheless. For years after that, he often thought that if he got rich and had himself a big plantation, he'd behave like Curtis and go around the country insisting on fair dealing for orphans and widow-women and such other misfortunate folk.

But now everything had changed. Now it was Bridgeman's task to ruin men of property. Since coming into the valley he burned every house he'd come to. Some of them had belonged to men he remembered—Ledbetter's on Shooting Creek, Penland's above Muskrat, Galloway's on the ridge below Ash Knob, Jarrett's at the head of the Licklog. Grasping, envious, wry-necked peckerwoods like Ryder, every one. He had burnt Ryder's place too, although Ryder was long dead. The place had smelt of the sour old son-of-a-bitch yet. Still, Old Man Curtis claimed to be a tory. Bridgeman didn't know whether to believe him, and anyway, till now the Yellow Jackets had made no such nice distinctions. Yet Bridgeman felt himself under something of an obligation. His mind turned back to the notion of a testing. Yes, he'd put Curtis's virtue to the test. Curtis was a justice of the peace and knew the condition of every man in the county. If in order to save his home Curtis could be made to betray neighbors he knew to be secesh, it would ease Bridgeman some; he could burn the old man out in good conscience despite the debt he owed him.

"I'll strike a bargain with you, Judge," Bridgeman said. "Give me the names of them in this valley as favors the rebels, and while me and the boys'll still rob your best goods, we'll pledge to leave this fine mansion of yours unburnt."

Curtis went pale and recoiled as if Bridgeman had struck him. "You say you know me, yet you take me for a rascal low enough to inform on his neighbors." He stood there shaking with indignation. "Sir," he cried, "you are gravely mistaken."

"If you're a union man like you claim," said Bridgeman, "it would be the act of a patriot to give up these rebels."

"Rebels or not," Curtis protested, "they're my neighbors and I won't turn on them."

Bridgeman shrugged. "I'll admit informing don't seem your style, Judge, given the lofty reputation you promote. But then, it's a grand home you've got here. Why, I watched you build it with your own hands, sweating right alongside your own nigras as if you was a nigra yourself. I expect it holds a good many dear memories. And sentiment apart, times are hard, there's the war, winter's coming on. A man needs a roof over his head, shelter for his wife and younguns." He gave Curtis a dry smile. "It ain't no ordinary choice I'm offering."

"Burn me out and be damned," Curtis exclaimed, folding his arms in a gesture of obstinance. "I'll not play the Judas." Grim-faced, his woman backed up towards the front door as if she thought to bar them entering with nothing but her tiny self. Liver and Lights and Bloody Bob and some of the others were already at the woodpile selecting lightwood that would serve for torches.

From the foot of the steps Porcupine eagerly spoke up. "Let's try that old Home Guard trick on him."

Bridgeman inclined his head in Porcupine's direction. "My man refers to a method of persuasion your rebel Home Guard liked to apply to folk that was with the union, up in

Mitchell County, before the Home Guard was all taken into the army."

"You mean torture," said Curtis.

"Yes, I do."

"Well, you can do your worst," the old man announced. "You'll not break me."

Bridgeman wagged his head in admiration. "I believe you, Judge," he said. "But what if we was to put Granny here to the ordeal?"

Old Man Curtis got very still and stern, but all he said was, "If you're contemptible enough to torment an innocent woman, I expect you couldn't break her, neither." For her part, Granny only lifted her chin an inch or two and gazed defiantly into Bridgeman's eyes, showing him that the prospect of mistreatment didn't scare her worth a damn. A certain amount of exasperation began to eat away at his good will, but all the same, their pluck had stirred his sporting blood. He felt they had engaged him in a contest. He beckoned to her, "Come here, Granny."

She crossed the gallery without looking even once at Old Man Curtis, and Bridgeman cupped a hand under her elbow and escorted her down the steps. Porcupine ran ahead of them to the worm fence, where he and Nix lifted the top rail out of its cradles and stood eagerly holding it as they approached. Stiffly, Old Man Curtis descended from the gallery and followed them. His face had turned bright red. Bloody Bob and Liver and Lights and the others had gathered around the place in the fence where the rail had been taken out, but they opened up a lane for the old man to walk through. He came and stood right beside the woman but did not touch her. She stood gazing calmly up the hill towards the woods beyond the road. Bridgeman needed to disturb the flinty

composure she and the old man were sharing. It had begun
to make him feel oddly inferior even as it aroused his respect.
"Kneel down," he ordered her, "and put your hands over that
second rail."

She obliged him without hesitating, though because of
her rheumatism she had to let herself down slow, steadying
herself by holding on to the fence. When she was in position,
Bridgeman nodded to Porcupine and Nix. Grinning, they
slid the top rail endwise through the cradles and set it down
on the one she was holding, with her fingers in between the
two. "Who's our rail-walker?" Bridgeman inquired. To the
cheers of the Yellow Jackets, Porcupine mounted the fence
quick as a monkey and stepped down on the rail he and Nix
had lowered and walked back and forth on it, jouncing his
weight up and down. An involuntary bleat escaped the
woman and her shoulders writhed in pain, but she said nothing. Old Man Curtis seemed to be looking the other way,
down the swale in the direction of the river. He had begun to
sweat. Porcupine did another turn. The woman moaned.
But the Yellow Jackets had been expecting more of a show
than this and now their shouting died away and they watched
in disappointed silence. One or two of them wandered off.
Porcupine teetered, recovered his balance, and walked the
rail again. This time he stopped in the middle, just over the
place where her fingers were caught, and jumped especially
hard. She yelped and then shook her head angrily as if to
reprove herself for giving voice.

"The Quillens," Old Man Curtis said. "Over on Sweetwater."

Bridgeman turned and gave him an inquiring look. It was
too good to be true. "What did you say?"

Awkwardly the woman twisted her head around in an

angry effort to catch sight of the old man. "You hush up, James Madison Curtis," she demanded. "I'm a-standing this just fine."

The old man ignored her. "Family name of Quillen on Sweetwater," he repeated. "They're secesh. And a family name of Puckett too, up on Fires Creek." Bridgeman came close and watched him to determine if he seemed sincere. "They've been raiding those of us that hold to the union, and they've got a great lot of goods. Livestock, silverware, china, specie. The wealth of every loyalist in the district." While he spoke, the old man's face was empty of any expression at all and his eyes, though they were set on Bridgeman, seemed to be looking into a far distance.

Bridgeman had never heard of any Pucketts but half-recalled the Quillens, a slovenly clan of po'-buckra that lived in a collection of miserable shacks up on the little pine mountain between Peachtree Creek and Sweetwater. They'd married their cousins till they all had yellow eyes and slack jaws. He couldn't remember their politics but doubted they'd have much in common with the Confederacy, being wholly without nigras and any property to speak of, except for the ten acres or so of stumpy hillside where they scratched out their thin living. Of course poverty didn't necessarily signify; the rebel army was full of fellows that hadn't a tin pot to call their own but had gone to war to fend off Yank coercion. Still, it was easier to imagine a Quillen given over to banditry for its own sake than to conceive of one wearing the gray out of principle. But it was even easier to imagine a Quillen cleaving to union for spite of such grandees as the Curtises, in whose shadow they'd lived for generations, and playing the tory guerrilla against them. Bridgeman concluded that Old Man Curtis was diddling him.

But he let Granny loose from the fence anyhow. After all,

the old man had passed Bridgeman's test. He had kept his virtue, and it pleased Bridgeman that Curtis had done it by telling an artful and elegant lie. Bridgeman approved of that. It amused him to think how neatly the old man was using his lie to turn the Yellow Jackets on those Quillens. The one part of the lie that was most likely true was the part about the Quillens robbing their neighbors and hoarding a big cache of stolen goods. Bridgeman guessed they'd cleaned out Curtis himself, and this was his way of getting back at them. It didn't matter a damn to Bridgeman if the Quillens worshipped Jeff Davis or Old Abe—not if they were holding treasure he could rob.

He sent Granny into the house to fetch out the rest of the relations. What emerged was a flock of womenfolk and children, including a pair of young wives with babes in arms and two queer boys that dressed and acted just alike. Some of the girls were fussing over Granny's hands but impatiently she waved them off. Bridgeman made the whole crowd of them sit in a bunch on the front steps while the Yellow Jackets went through the house. They watched patiently and without complaint while the boys trooped past, toting candlesticks, oil paintings, samplers, quilts, salt meat from the attic, rugs, a hat rack made of deer antlers, a terra-cotta umbrella stand. A Newfoundland dog came in from the fields with beggar-lice all over it and ran around in a fit of excitement barking at the boys as they worked. Presently the noise grew tiresome and Nix shot it. Not even then did any of the Curtises protest, though some of the least ones commenced to cry.

When they were done, Bloody Bob struck a match to his lightwood and was fixing to set the house afire when Bridgeman stopped him. "I pledged my word to this old man," he explained.

Bloody Bob gaped. A third eye might as well have appeared in the middle of Bridgeman's forehead. When at last his astonishment allowed him to catch his breath, he cried, "Hell, Colonel, it don't mean nothing now."

"It does if I say it does, Bob," Bridgeman replied. He drew his Remington New Model Army revolver and cocked it and put the snout of it against Bob's head and Bob blew out his lightwood.

When they were ready to go, with the column formed up and the stolen plow horse harnessed to the Judge's buggy and all the Curtises' goods stacked inside and Ledbetter at the reins, Bridgeman rode up the walk between the boxwoods to the foot of the front steps where the old man stood, still wearing his stovepipe hat and frock coat, with his family gathered close about him. Bridgeman doffed his cap to him and said, "You don't know it, Judge, but I owed you a favor from long ago and after a good deal of thought, I decided to repay it today. But you and me are quits now. When I come through here again, things may be different."

Old Man Curtis made no reply, just stood there looking up at him full of the virtue that Bridgeman had tried and failed to soil. Yes, Bridgeman had made him lie. But the sort of lie he told had actually been a kind of truth. Bridgeman thought about this and became aware that if the old man's behavior had pleased and amused him, it had mortified him too. It was good to have it confirmed that Curtis was the man of quality he remembered. But in proving his quality Curtis had also shown how base was Bridgeman himself. Dismally, Bridgeman saw that he could hope to come no nearer than the hated Frank Ryder could, to such quality as that. This was a woeful rediscovery of something he had known when he lived with Ryder but had been trying hard to forget ever since.

Angrily he whirled his gelding and broke down part of the boxwood hedge and rode across the yard to the head of the column, and then with a hoarse yell he led the Yellow Jackets at a canter through the gate in the fence and up the lane to the road, where two of the boys had been holding the livestock. There they all turned west, towards Fires Creek and Sweetwater.

Chapter Four

❂ ❂ ❂

1

Chilled to the bone, Andy lay shivering on the parlor settee. He was still covered with the cloak and shawl Salina had wrapped around him to keep out the springhouse damp. Now Betty spread over him Sarah's heavy knitted afghan, while Sarah herself stood anxiously by, her injured hands curled at her bosom like implements she had lost interest in using but had forgotten to lay aside. Her knuckles had swollen alarmingly, and although she made no complaint, the others could see that her fingers were in a bad way. Martha was in the summer kitchen making up poultices smeared with petroleum jelly and crushed fern leaves, to ease the pain Sarah was suffering but refused to admit to.

Betty stood back and turned a wondering gaze around the room. Broken china littered the floor; a chandelier pulled out of the dining room ceiling and thrown into the parlor lay by the hearth in a scatter of crystal fragments; the window-lights had been broken out. "Bless the Lord," she said. "It's a miracle they spared us the house."

"And a miracle they made no search of the grounds," Sarah added, gazing thankfully down on Andy.

The younger children were in the yard, the Cartman boys and Jack's Alec were rushing about imitating the depradations of the partisans, while the girls inspected the dead Newfoundland, the overturned privy, the ransacked corncrib, and the shambles that had been made of the boxwoods, the crape myrtle, the woodpile. Salina sat lank-haired and pale in the rocker next to the settee, her skirts smeared with red mud from the springhouse floor. Mary paced up and down with Martha's Eva nestled in the bend of one arm and her own little Sarah in the other.

Madison shuttled between the settee and the front doorway, alternately watching over Andy in the parlor and hurrying into the entry to scan the outdoors in case the bushwhackers took a notion to return and fire the house after all, the way that little fellow with the red beard had wanted. But the landscape lay silent now except for an occasional crackle of small-arms fire in the distance, and if the sunlight had a dim, sepia look because of the smoke and dust hanging in the air, still the day felt fresh and bright to Madison because of their deliverance. He still cradled the rifle in one arm and he leaned the shotgun by the door, but it did seem that Betty was right, God had somehow intervened to preserve them. How else explain the odd forbearance of the leader of the partisans, the one in the yellow blouse they called the Colonel, who said so mysteriously that he owed Madison a debt?

After they rode out, Madison had stripped off his coat, heavy with his own fear-sweats, and hung it on a wall-peg and he unbuttoned his damp waistcoat to find his linen shirt soaked too and his collar wilted and his cravat hanging limp with wet. The inside of his hat, when he removed it, was greasy and stank, his fringe of hair was a thin ring of sodden curls that only now had begun to cool. He had been frightened nearly to death when they put Sarah down on the ground with her hands in that fence. Returning to the parlor, he met Sarah's gaze and held it for a long moment full of much unspoken thought. Then Betty said to Andy, "You should've seen the grit your mama showed those brutes."

Andy rolled a despairing look towards Sarah. "Lord, I hate it that such dangers can come down on you. Did they hurt you terrible, Mama?"

Martha came in from the summer kitchen and began to bind Sarah's hands with the poultices. Dismissively Sarah replied, "I've hurt myself worse fixing dinner."

Suddenly Betty laughed in that brazen way she had. "You also should have seen Mama tell Papa to hush up."

A disapproving look came over Madison and he decided to go back into the entry and check outside for returning bandits. Sarah blushed a deep crimson but it was easy to see that she had enjoyed Betty's remark, and as Martha helped her into the armchair she explained how she worried that Father Curtis might be tempted to give up their friends, just to stop her suffering. "I'd never have spoke so sharp, otherwise," she said, demurely.

Weakly Andy smiled. "What'd you say to him, Mama?"

Sarah colored an even deeper scarlet. "Why, I don't recollect exactly."

"I do," cried Betty. "I was standing right by the door and heard every word. You said, 'You hush up, James Madison Curtis. I'm a-standing this just fine.'"

The parlor rocked with laughter. Genuinely alarmed, Sarah raised a bandaged hand to her mouth. "Did I? Surely I didn't."

Madison had come back into the room. He stood by the settee frowning and chewing the end of his mustache. Clearly in their relief at being delivered from the rangers, his family had put by their customary decorum. He was unsure how to restore it. The outspoken Betty seemed to be the source of the mischief. He was still trying to think of a way to reprove her without seeming unduly harsh when Betty made an even more remarkable sally. "And Papa told a lie, too," she burst out. "After insisting all our lives it's a sin to tell a falsehood, he swore to that bushwhacker we were for the union and the Quillens and the Pucketts were secesh."

In the awkward stillness that greeted this remark, Betty's whoop of glee echoed emptily; all the others were observing Madison guardedly. The fun had subsided once they called to mind his famous dignity. Now Betty's boldness seemed to come near mocking him. They sat seized with the fearful knowledge that they had become too familiar. He felt their wariness like a change in the weather, and at the same time he glanced at Sarah and saw how steadily she was regarding him.

A look like that from Sarah was always enough to make him stop and take thought. He saw at once that he ought not chasten them, but could not think what was right to do. He supposed humor was in order, but he had never been able to laugh. The most he could get out of himself when he felt merry was a sort of choking noise at the back of his throat. But he did have a habit of running his forefinger under his mustache when something inordinantly pleased him, and it was a gesture they all recognized. He did this now, and said, "Well, I expect a body can always lie to a thieving Yankee, without the Lord charging it to his account."

It wasn't much, but it was enough to lighten the mood of the room. They laughed, though assuredly more politely than before, and if Betty was now wearing the stubborn look she always wore when she thought Madison had carried his reserve too far, she turned brightly enough to Andy and asked him how he enjoyed his sojourn in the springhouse.

Andy shuddered. He had lain on his back on a pallet of straw Salina and Betty and his father had spread for him in the small space of packed earth beside the spring. Next to him, in the cooling trough over the live water, were stoneware jugs of milk and crocks of butter beaded with moisture. There was a crawfish at the bottom of the spring that he could see if he half rolled over and raised his head. It scuttled back and forth over the pale pebbles, its image distorted by the wrinkling eddies. He lay grasping the big Harpers Ferry pistol in both hands under his swaddling of blanket and quilt. Salina was crouched by the door with the shotgun across her lap and the rifle propped against the wall behind her. The door was ajar, and through it she kept watch up the ravine. He admired the clean line of her profile and thought how brave she was. Bill Cartman's Newfoundland dog kept trying to get into the springhouse till Salina poked it in the snout with the shotgun and it squealed and ran off. Sunlight streamed through the gap in the door and reflected off the water and turned the satiny old browns and tans of the plank walls into a shimmer of gold. The cobwebs in the corners undulated slowly in the warm drafts. A big speckled spider was patiently spinning a web between the rafters. Dirt-daubers came and went. The chill of the water searched the marrow of his bones. He lay quaking and sweating and smelling his own stench, mortified to be inflicting on sweet Salina the unholy odor of his afflicted bowels. But the worst of it was the waiting and the not knowing, especially after they heard the pistol shot. It had seemed hours and hours before his father jerked open the door to flood the springhouse with blinding light and thrust his grinning head inside.

He sent Betty a wan smile. "Why, we had us a fine time,

lying there half the day waiting for a pack of murderers to bust in on us and drag me out by the heels and hang me to the limb of a tree." Then he looked sad. "I just wish we could've made a fight of it somehow. I can't hardly stand the thought of those rascals doing hurt to Mama."

"Don't you fret, Andy," Sarah spoke up. "They only mashed my knuckles some. The rheumatism itself hurts me worse, some days. Anyhow, I believe it was worth a dab of discomfort to send down tribulation on those Quillens and Pucketts." That fetched another laugh from everyone but Madison, who wore a troubled air as he began to ponder the consequences of the lie he had told the Yankee officer. But even though he laughed, Andy grimly reflected how far this war had got beyond what anybody had expected when it started. Who could tell what terrible lengths it might go to before it ever came to an end? It was unimaginable how the war could have commenced in a dispute over high principle and then two years later descend to the point that a scurvy crowd of villains could ride into his own dooryard, vandalize his home, and put his precious mama to torture.

There was a clamor on the gallery. The two Cartman boys came pounding inside on bare feet. In the parlor archway they stopped and yelled in unison, "Grandpa, there's a soldier coming!"

2

"I declare, Miz Barter," he boomed as Martha rose from the table to gather up their plates, "this was the grandest meal I've consumed since my own dear mama made me a special feast the day I left home for the war." Already they had grown used to his exaggerated way of speaking. It was plain he only meant to please.

"Roast turkey," he cried, recounting the wonders of that going-away banquet down in Georgia a year ago last March, "giblet gravy, mashed potatoes, candied yams, mince pie, biscuits three inches tall, with just the merest flake of crust and the insides fluffy as so much fine-ginned cotton." It did not occur to him that his catalog of mouth-watering delicacies only served to emphasize how meager had been the fare that Martha, under the injured Sarah's direction, had managed to scrape together from the few scraps the raiders had overlooked—bacon fat, Irish potatoes, boiled cabbage. "'Course you don't know my mama," he went on expansively, "so you can't appreciate the honor I'm doing you, but you may trust me that these here eats today was just as grand as anything she could have rustled up."

He was a talker, this Oliver Price. From the moment Madison had shown him into the parlor he'd been prattling on in his large voice, greeting Andy with roars of enthusiasm that quickly changed to groans of solicitude once he saw that Andy was ill, loudly regaling them with the story of his near-encounter with the bushwhackers; condemning the scoundrels for their mistreatment of Sarah; exuberantly praising the mild temper of the infants, the good looks of the Curtis girls; Alec's ability to dash about so nimbly, and what he called the "right particular resemblance" of the two Cartman boys.

Endlessly he extolled the land. "No matter it's ravaged and untended on account of the disturbed times, a man can see the bounty it'll bear when peace comes. Buckwheat, oats, barley, rye, wheat, corn, timothy clover, tobacco, apples, huckleberries . . ." He went on and on, while they sat compliantly nodding amid the exuberant torrent of words.

Now as they left the supper table and returned to the parlor where Andy lay resting on the settee, Oliver began to

expand on how he had met Andy and Jack in the summer of
'62 in East Tennessee. "Everybody was sick that spring. Half
my regiment was in the hospital over at Knoxville with the
measles, pneumonia, rheumatism, camp fever, whooping
cough. I don't expect the whole of Stevenson's division had
a thousand men fit for duty. You couldn't hear the sergeants
giving orders for the sound of men a-coughing. I'd always
been healthy as a mule and they made me orderly to Reynolds, our brigade commander, on account of his orderly
being sick. And one night Reynolds sent me over to the 39th
North Carolina with a dispatch for Colonel Coleman, and
Andy was acting orderly-sergeant, and Jack was there too
spending the night, and after I delivered my dispatch, we fell
to talking.

"I'll never forget how it struck me when they talked of
home. Now any man is fond of his home and will speak good
of it. But these two boys was rapturous. In my mind's eye I
could see the valley with the mountains set all about it, the
herds grazing on the balds, the crops standing thick, the
creeks running fresh out of the highlands. Now Rabun Gap,
which is my home, is pleasant enough country, but it seemed
like Andy and Jack was telling of the Garden of Eden. I was
born in Carolina myself, in Rutherford County yonside the
Blue Ridge, but we went into Georgia when I was just a shirt-
tail youngster, so I had no notion of Carolina beyond going
down to Franklin to market now and then, never been west
of the Nantahalas."

He had fine sandy hair that lay close to his head, deep-set
brown eyes, and cheekbones as sharp as an Indian's. He wore
a walrus mustache that concealed his mouth. His hands were
small and looked surprisingly delicate. He was a medium-
sized man who seemed larger than he was because his
uniform of brownish-gray homespun was too small for him

Blessed are ye that weep now: for ye shall laugh.
Blessed are ye, when men shall hate you, and
    when they shall separate you from their
    company, and shall reproach you, and cast out
    your name as evil, for the Son of man's sake.
Rejoice ye in that day, and leap for joy: for, behold,
    your reward is great in heaven: for in like
    manner did their fathers unto the prophets.

Oliver closed the little book, and they all said, "Amen," in unison.

That night before going to bed, Oliver walked out on the upper gallery and stood looking up at the millions of stars spread over the dark canopy of sky. It was a moonless night and he could just make out the black contours of the mountains in the distance. He listened to the song of the crickets winding through the dark, and somewhere close by there was a whipporwill. Otherwise, the land lay wrapped in utter stillness. At that moment it was hard to believe that evil men were at large and a terrible war was raging. The peace here was too profound, it was holy. Madison had told him that when he first came into the valley, he could feel God around him. Oliver felt that now. He knelt down on the gallery and folded his hands on the railing and prayed. He thanked the Lord for leading him home.

Chapter Five

❂ ❂ ❂

1

In the unseasonably chilly weather that had closed in during the night, they ascended the narrow drainage between the Tusquittees on their right hand and the Valley River range that soared higher and higher on their left, till the crown of its summit, Big Peachtree Bald, was lost in lowering clouds.

The narrow, seldom-traveled path led them up through thickets of dogwood and sumac and rhododendron, and above them on the higher slopes rose a ragged growth of hickory, black walnut, and oak. Further up, the mountain was clothed with pine marred here and there by ugly brownish-black deadfalls where plagues of insect borers had killed masses of trees.

The track climbed steeply, leaving Fires Creek tumbling far below in a creamy froth around the big, smooth streambed rocks that years of weathering had bleached white. When there were breaks in the undergrowth, they could see the green slopes of the Tusquittees across the way, partially veiled in mist, rising in folds to where the flat line of cloud cut off their tops. The road itself was badly eroded, and the horses kept stumbling in the deep ruts. "God damn this bloody pig-path to hell," cried Nix when his mount lunged sideways in a pothole and nearly pitched him headlong into the abyss. "If there's a cache of goods on this mountain, it damn well better be a rich un."

"There ain't no damn goods," Liver and Lights angrily predicted. "If we had to leave all our truck below, how d'ye reckon a pack of robbers could fetch wagonloads of goods 'long here?"

Bloody Bob snorted in disgust. "That old planter misdirected us, I'm a-thinking." He cast an evil eye at Bridgeman's back. "We ought to have burnt him out."

Bridgeman checked his gelding, slewed in the saddle and fixed Bob with a hard look while the column came to a halt behind him, all zigzagged on the twisting path. "If you want to dispute me again," he told Bob in a pleasant tone, "you'd best come at me a-smoking, and hit me the first pull. Otherwise, hush up. I ain't killed anybody all day." He'd been in a vicious temper ever since leaving the Curtis place the day before. Bob ventured no more comment, and they resumed their tedious climb. In another twenty minutes a thin, drizzly rain commenced, and the chill worsened till horses and men were blowing plumes of vapor with every breath. Their clothes dark with damp, they bowed their shoulders against the rain as it quickly turned from a blowing mist to a downpour.

Presently they got to a place where the creek came down between banks choked with laurel and fern, where a long time ago several big trees had fallen crosswise over the streambed and mistletoe had covered the rotting trunks, so the creek ran through a sort of low tunnel of vegetation. Then it came out, smelling of moss, dimpled by the rain, and, dividing around a scatter of big rocks, sorted itself into a number of thick braids clear as glass and hurtled over a ledge, dropping in a roaring cascade two hundred feet into a cloud of spray that hovered perpetually down below.

Bridgeman led them upstream from the falls to a place where they could ford, and they crossed under a large poplar tree that sheltered them briefly from the rain and then they struggled up a muddy, shelving bank through tangles of blackberry and sassafras that drenched them even more with cold wet. They emerged in a grassy meadow. At the end of the meadow was a line of woods with a rude cabin made of squared logs backed into it behind a stake-and-rail fence entwined with grapevine, and beyond this, the timbered mountainside. Huddled about the cabin were a chicken coop, a corn crib, a privy, and a well house. Off to the side there was an old log barn half fallen in. They were so near the clouds now that all the distances were obscured by fog. Tendrils of cloud clung to the woods. The rain started to let up.

Bridgeman was about to order Porcupine and Liver and Lights to go reconnoiter the house when a man with a long bushy beard, wearing a blue cavalry overcoat and a slouch hat, stepped around the end of the barn carrying a musket. He cupped a hand next to his mouth and hollered, "You boys with the Union?"

It hardly mattered what Bridgeman said. "Sure enough," he cried. "We're Bridgeman's Yellow Jackets, raiding out of Cosby, Tennessee."

"Like hell," declared the fellow. He leveled his musket, and when he fired, powder also flared at a half-dozen other places along the vine-covered fence, and Nix seized his throat with crossed hands and toppled off his horse into a patch of wild strawberries and lay there with blood spouting out between his fingers. The Yellow Jackets replied with a spatter of pistol fire, but because of the damp weather, the smoke from the Pucketts' first volley had settled in a dirty gray bank to conceal the fence and the men behind it. So rather than go to ground and waste time with long-range skirmishing, the Yellow Jackets just shook themselves into a crooked line and made a whooping horseback charge on the fence.

They lost four more crossing the meadow, including Porcupine. Bloody Bob killed the fellow by the barn. Bridgeman jumped his gelding over the fence and rode down the fence line shooting them from behind, and dropped two before a third one shot his horse and brought him down on the doorstone of the cabin. This enraged Bridgeman because he fancied that piebald gelding beyond all reason. When the shooting stopped, Bridgeman took the man who had killed his horse and hanged him from the limb of a chestnut tree by the cabin with a length of plowline. After that, there was one Puckett left alive, except for the womenfolk they found hiding in the house. He was a skinny boy with yellow buck teeth and big white-headed pimples all over his face. Liver and Lights worked on him with a skinning knife till he told where the goods were hidden, then Bridgeman hanged him too, next to the first one.

They left the old granny and the young woman groaning over their dead. They followed a weedy lane into the woods and up the side of the mountain among rocks and holly thickets and sand myrtle bushes. The entrance to the cave was an inauspicious little cleft between two boulders, hardly wide enough for a man to pass without turning his shoulders to one side. Bloody Bob had brought some shucks and once inside he struck a light. Several timber rattlers buzzed lazily and then went winding out of sight. Judge Curtis may have lied about the Pucketts being secesh, but he had told the truth about their loot. There were candelabras tarnished black, stacks of fine bone china, sacks of silver flatware, rows of crystal goblets full of spiders' nests, oil portraits covered with mold, calfskin-bound Bibles with gilt-edged pages, chests of jewelry and coin, an unabridged dictionary green with mildew, a tea-service splattered with bat-droppings, a guitar with mother-of-pearl inlay.

2

If Bridgeman had somehow been able to cross the divide of the Valley River range near Pucketts' and follow Peachtree Creek down to its mouth on the Hiwassee, instead of having to descend Fires Creek the way he came, he could have reached Sweetwater from the rear, and made a shorter trip of it. But he didn't know a pass over the mountains, and anyway he had no choice in the matter: He had left a party of men on Tusquittee guarding the livestock and plunder.

So he began to pick his way back down the rutted path. It was slow going because of the bad road and because each of them was carrying some of the Pucketts' treasure. The goods were loose-packed and prone to shift, and the racket made the horses nervous. The rain had stopped, but the wet red clay of the road was slippery. Partway down, Ledbetter's horse broke a foreleg and fell floundering on the edge of the road with the soft ground crumbling away underneath it, dropping clods and stones a long way into the treetops down below. Ledbetter's leg was caught underneath the horse and the rest of him dangled in space while the big poke he'd been carrying came loose and fell thirty feet before it struck an outcrop and exploded in a shower of serving platters and candlesticks. Presently a great chunk of earth gave way and Ledbetter and the horse fell free.

It was nightfall of the tenth day of their raid when they rejoined the party they had left on Tusquittee. The next morning dawned gray and cool but there was no rain. They set out for Sweetwater. So far Bridgeman had lost seven men in action: Fly-Speck in the Cowees, Porcupine and four others at Pucketts', Ledbetter on the road down. Three of his casualties at Pucketts' farm had been wounded and he'd left them wailing where they fell. He didn't want to think what those Puckett womenfolk had done to them by now. Six men had deserted somewhere along the way, and two had fallen out sick. He had thirty-five with him when he crossed the broad bottom of the Hiwassee at Sweetwater. But it took a dozen men to look after the livestock and drive the buggy and two wagons they had taken to tote the plunder in. So he had twenty-three Yellow Jackets with him when he rode up to the Quillens'.

When it was over, he had twenty-two. Not because of a fight—there wasn't any; the place was deserted—but because Bridgeman finally lost patience with Bloody Bob, who cursed him when they discovered the Quillens had skedaddled with all the goods. "You dumb son-of-a-bitch," Bob was howling, "that old planter made a goddamn fool of you." He meant to say more but Bridgeman shot him before he could finish.

Even without any plunder from the Quillens, Bridgeman felt he had done well in the Hiwassee valley. Yes, it still rankled him that Old Man Curtis had got the better of him. But he had evened the debt he owed the judge, and he had burnt the stench of Frank Ryder out of his nostrils, and he had sure as hell made those dirt-eater Clay County farmers howl. And the whole of Cherokee County lay before him yet.

What Bridgeman didn't know was that somebody else had already got into Cherokee ahead of him. This was Captain Goldman Bryson and a hundred and fifty of what he called the 1st Tennessee National Guard. General Burnside, now at Knoxville, had given Bryson the orders Bridgeman had been pretending to have received, to go into the highlands and lend support to the tories. Bryson may have carried official orders, but he was no more legitimate than Bridgeman. For some days he'd been ravaging everything, tory and secesh alike, from Bear Paw down to Murphy and the watershed of the Nottely. To counter him, Bragg at Chattanooga had sent over a detachment of cavalry under Brigadier General John C. Vaughn.

At the same time, some of the Thomas Legion had come in at last from Valleytown. Watson Curtis's message warning of Bridgeman's raid had reached Colonel Will Thomas there within hours of an appeal from Vaughn for reinforcements against Bryson. Thomas sent down Company B of the Legion, a hundred and twenty-three redskins, under the command of a halfbreed, Lieutenant Campbell Taylor. Between them, Vaughn's cavalry and Taylor's Cherokee infantry had scattered the Bryson people. Bryson himself was dead by the time Bridgeman and the Yellow Jackets approached Murphy from the direction of Sweetwater.

Bridgeman made camp on the Hiwassee outside of Murphy and, even though he could hear a crackle of firing off to the west, he neglected to send out scouts or even set up a picket. He was confident that a command the size of the Yellow Jackets had little to fear from the parties of scavenging deserters he believed had done the shooting. It wasn't long before the Legion found him. They hit the camp at dawn. They came dodging through the poplars in their plumed turbans, howling like mad wolves. Some had on Confederate uniforms but others were stripped down to their breechclouts and wore paint on their faces. Bridgeman and the Yellow

Jackets formed a ring and fought off two attacks before full daylight, when the Cherokee drew back to dance and smoke and sing war-songs. Bridgeman lost three men, one of whom was dragged off screaming by a pair of warriors and later found in the woods, scalped but alive. Bridgeman left him as he was, and presently formed the column and led it south up the Nottely, sending the drove of livestock and train of goods ahead of him. Oddly the redskins, who had it in their power to massacre the lot of them, now behaved as though the Yellow Jackets had ceased to exist. As Bridgeman headed out, they were playing a game of ball on the riverbank.

By nightfall of the twelfth day, he had turned west along the road that would take him over the Stansburys towards Ducktown on the Ocoee, in Tennessee. From there he aimed to strike the line of the Tennessee and Georgia Railroad and follow it northeast behind the Unicois up to Knoxville and Cosby. He made camp on Wolf Creek just a mile or two short of the state line. It was a cold night, with a misty rain falling. In the dreary weather Bridgeman began to feel disconsolate. The livestock and goods were impeding his march, and his throat was sore and he was tired and wished to be finished with this expedition. He hadn't liked running into those redskins. He kept remembering the peeled skull of the scalped man.

At sunup he found that one of his wounded from the fuss at Murphy had died in the night, and he had him laid by the road, on the even chance that some Good Samaritan would find and bury him before the buzzards or a drove of hogs did. But it was Vaughn's cavalry that came across him, an hour after Bridgeman had taken the road into Tennessee. At a place just outside of Ducktown where the road went through a grove of ash and red oak, Vaughn pitched into the livestock which was again traveling at the rear of Bridgeman's column.

At once the woods were full of cows, mules, sheep, oxen, horses, and goats running in all directions. Liver and Lights, who was driving the Curtises' buggy, managed to get away with its load of goods, but Vaughn captured the two wagons heaped with the Puckett treasure and all the valuables the Yellow Jackets had collected in four counties.

Bridgeman put up as much of a fight as he could before taking to his heels with nineteen of his men and Liver and Lights in the buggy. A raging thunderstorm discouraged the pursuit.

Chapter Six

❀ ❀ ❀

Oliver Price considered himself as good a Christian as the next man. But in his opinion, what Judge Curtis had decided to do about the Quillens went far beyond Christianity. He supposed it was an act of righteousness—Jesus said to love your enemies, after all—but it was hard to see how a man who'd suffered what the judge had suffered at the hands of the Quillens could feel bound to give them notice of the bushwhackers.

"I can't do anything about the Pucketts," the judge had lamented, after rapping urgently on the door of the pantry where Oliver was sleeping and entering in a state of high agitation. "Whatever has become of them will be on my head. God will judge me for it at the Last Day. But at least I can save the Quillens."

Over supper, Oliver had listened in horror to the judge's account of the depradations of the tories. With his own eyes he'd seen the ruin they visited on the Curtis plantation. Now he could scarcely believe his ears as the judge spoke of regaining his peace of mind by preserving these same evildoers from the partisans. But what came next startled him even more. "You've said you must go on west tomorrow, through Murphy, to catch the cars at Chattanooga and rejoin your regiment. Your way will take you past the Quillens' farm. Will you give them a warning of the bushwhackers?"

Oliver sat up in his cot and regarded him as if he were a species of being he had never before encountered. Maybe he was. Anybody who could feel torment on account of having set one pack of scorpions on another could hardly be an ordinary human. "Judge," he said, "I'm obliged to you for your kindness and because of Andy and Jack, but, sir, I'm a Confederate States soldier and them folks is blue-dyed tories. I ain't aiming to weep none if they was to fall prey to that pack of scavengers." A note of reproach crept into his voice in spite of the deference he felt. "And I shouldn't think you'd want to, neither."

The judge sat down on the pantry stool and glared at the bare shelves opposite him. "I spoke in haste, to save my wife from the ordeal. I was willing to sacrifice others to protect my own."

Oliver rested a hand on the bony round of the old man's shoulder. "That ain't a sin, Judge. It's what folks do, when they're pressed by malefactors."

"My conscience won't let me rest," the judge declared. "Tonight, after everything quietened down, I commenced studying on what I'd done, and I saw that I couldn't live with it." He looked up at Oliver and his rugged face was set in a way Oliver had not seen before. "It'll be done, Mr Price. The question is, who's to do it. Andy can't; he's too poorly. If you won't, then I will."

"You've got no mount," Oliver pointed out, "and you can't walk it." It sounded to Oliver as if his courage was being questioned, or maybe his honor. At first he felt as if he ought to take offense, but one glance at the pain in the old man's eyes changed his temper entirely, and something like shame came over him. The judge only wanted to do right. "How far is it from here to the Quillens'?"

"Ten, twelve miles by the roads. There's a shorter way, but you wouldn't know it."

Oliver shook his head. "That's half a day's walking. Would I be in time?"

"The turnoff to the Pucketts' is nearest. The bushwhackers will have gone there first, and it's a bad road up Fires Creek and back. They'll be at it all day. They won't get to Sweetwater before morning of the day after tomorrow." He fixed his eyes on Oliver again; Oliver had seen a saucer of Wedgwood china once, in a shop in Clayton, and its blue was the same as the blue in the judge's eyes. He was a strong man and a good one, but hard. Oliver saw now why Andy and Jack both feared and loved him.

The judge extended his big-knuckled, bent-fingered hand and Oliver shook it, feeling the rasp of its calluses. "I'm obliged to you for this, Mr Price," the judge said sternly; he was moved but dared not show it. "I believe you're a man of character. When the war's over, I hope you'll do what you said and come into this valley and farm. I'd be pleased to be your neighbor." Embarrassed, he stood up immediately and started out, then paused at the door. "We'll rise at dawn, and I'll direct you to the Quillens'."

Events, it seemed, were drawing Oliver closer and closer to the Curtises. The judge, Miz Curtis, the daughters, Andy's wife, all were of the finest sort; it was an honor to have won their trust and affection. But as he lay back on his cot, his thoughts returned to Jack and Andy, the first of the Curtises he knew, whom he had met by chance and so quickly come to admire. How had they earned his love? Why, they'd showed him respect. This was a large matter. Their natural station was high and his was low, yet they had offered him the friendship of equals. Now, here in their home, he could see where that kind of grace had come from. The judge dispensed it the way the sun shed its beams on the world.

Before going to bed that night he sat smoking his pipe by the settee where Andy was resting. They reminisced about their days in Stevenson's division and recounted where they had been since. Oliver told how his regiment had got sent to Mississippi and he stood the siege of Vicksburg and Pemberton had surrendered him and he lost Freddy. Andy said he and Jack had both laid out a spell last winter. Then they too had gone to Mississippi. The 39th North Carolina had been assigned to McNair's brigade of French's division, and had got sent to General Joe Johnston, first at Jackson, then at Canton, and finally at Birdsong's Farm, in the army that Johnston was assembling to relieve Pemberton at Vicksburg. "Why, Oliver," Andy cried, "we was trying to rescue you."

Oliver laughed his booming laugh. "Well, you was too late." Beneath their banter lay an uneasiness born of the knowledge that Oliver had seen a good deal of fighting while Andy and Jack had done little more than guard bridges and mountain passes, march and countermarch, and sit in camp. The one scrape of the Kentucky campaign, at Perryville, they all three had missed on account of Kirby Smith squatting on Bragg's right flank all day without attacking. But then Oliver had gone south and seen the elephant. Because of lying out last winter, Andy and Jack had missed the big scrap at Murfreesboro. The fact that Oliver had smelt powder and Andy hadn't, separated them in spite of their liking for each other. In the end, it made it hard for them to say much more that evening, and presently Oliver had told Andy goodnight and gone to bed in the pantry, where Miz Curtis had had the girls make up the cot for him. The distance he felt from Andy had troubled him, and kept him wakeful till the judge came tapping at his door.

The whole household rose before daybreak to bid him farewell. He took the liberty of fetching each of the women a brotherly buss on the cheek, and he hugged all the younger daughters right down to Rebecca, the least one. Soberly he shook hands with the Cartman boys in their identical sailor suits, then he chased Jack's Alec around the gallery. Andy came out, white as clabber and wearing his mama's shawl. "Maybe when I get over this," he said, "I'll see you at Chattanooga."

Oliver took his hand. "I expect Bragg won't be at Chattanooga a whole lot longer. At Franklin they told me Rosecrans was going into Georgia. Greet Jack for me, now."

Miz Curtis held her bandaged hands crosswise on her bosom. "Remember to take pen in hand to us, Mr Price. We'll be anxious to hear from you."

He promised to write. The judge gave him directions to the Quillens'. "Suppose they fight me and won't listen?" Oliver inquired. "And even if I get a hearing, suppose they won't believe me?"

The judge took him by the arm in a reassuring way. "They won't fight. They may be tories, but they pretend to cooperate with the Confederate authorities. Likely they'll bow and scrape to you." He handed Oliver a folded piece of ruled paper. Oliver opened it a ways and saw that there was writing on it. "There's one of them that can read," the judge said. "Old Mose, the head of the clan. You give him this."

Oliver took his leave of the Curtises just as the sun began to brighten the overcast above the Nantahalas. At the top of the lane he turned back to wave at them, but they'd all gone inside by then. He stood a moment taking in the view down to the river. Then he set off along the stony road towards the highroad.

It rained lightly at intervals all morning, and once he heard thunder rumbling up in the Tusquittees and saw a play of lightning among the peaks, but the storm passed off towards the east and he made good time on the highroad. In the moist air the smell of char was rank and bitter. Smoke lay in motionless white streamers close to the ground. Apart from the burnt-over places, the untended countryside had a shaggy, ramshackle look where the grass had run wild and the weeds and vines had taken over and the fences had fallen down. The scorched chimneys of burnt houses rose on every hand. Mower-blades and the tines of dump rakes rusted amid the fallen timbers of neglected barns. The few people he encountered on the road hurried past him with their eyes averted, fearing he meant them harm.

He reached the Quillens' turnoff in a misty drizzle some time past the middle of the day, and before he went up, he sat on a stone and ate the corn dodgers and fat meat Miz Barter had fixed him. Then he trudged up the steep lane cut deep with wagon ruts that wound through the scraggly pine woods to a cleared space studded with old stumps and covered with broken wheels, cracked jugs, broached barrels, coils of rotted rope, decayed horse-collars, hundreds of pieces of broken crockery. Up the littered slope, a windowless shack made of random planks and beams leaned crazily to one side. Its chimney was a wooden cask with both ends knocked out, and a thread of smoke issued out of it and flattened into a gauzy line. The piece of split deerhide hanging over the door parted and Old Mose Quillen came out, along with an ammoniac odor so strong it brought tears to Oliver's eyes.

The judge had been right; Old Mose was full of deference for the Confederate States uniform, and when Oliver gave him the folded note, he declared his gratitude to the heavens.

"Squire Curtis, now there's a godly man," he cried. "The milk of loving kindness flows in him, he's a fount of Christian charity, mercy rolls down like waters and righteousness like a mighty stream." Behind him as he declaimed appeared six or eight lanky, yellow-complexioned Quillens of indeterminate gender clad in dirty rags. Mose himself was as black as a nigra with grime, and wore a long beard clotted with matter Oliver had no wish to identify. The breath he expelled was like an exhalation from the nether regions.

His deed of mercy accomplished, Oliver declined Old Mose's invitation to sup with the family and made his way back down the path to the turnpike. By nightfall he was in Murphy. He found the place swarming with Cherokee from the Thomas Legion. They were celebrating the killing of a Yank bushwhacker named Bryson. Most of them were drunk. The drunk ones were shooting in the air and some of them were brandishing Bryson's blood-soaked trousers and jacket.

Oliver considered this a providential development. He scouted out the Cherokees' officer, a burly lieutenant named Taylor, who was the color of scorched copperware and had eyes with green lights in them like opals and wore a fierce mustache and imperial. Oliver told him about the bushwhackers up at Pucketts', who'd be coming towards Murphy from Sweetwater in the morning. Taylor expressed himself gratified to hear the news.

Not caring for the company of a pack of Cherokee wild with popskull, Oliver took supper in a tavern at the edge of town and inquired of the keeper the nearest way to Chattanooga. When he finished his meal, he walked a distance along the road the keeper had pointed out to him, till he found himself a cozy fence corner sheltered from the drizzle by a spruce tree. There he curled up and went to sleep, feeling fairly well satisfied with himself.

Chapter Seven

❁ ❁ ❁

It was bad enough that Confederate armies were getting turned out of Knoxville and Chattanooga both at once, so that the whole of East Tennessee was nothing but one great mass of troops and wagon trains clogging every southbound road, forcing the cavalry to shift for itself following farm lanes and pig-paths, or even going cross-country, which meant stopping every half-mile to throw down fences or look for a place to ford one of the innumerable streams that ran through this infernal country. No, as if this weren't a sufficiency of devilment, some fool in the Adjutant and Inspector General's Office had decided that the battalion ought to be reorganized, smack in the middle of the biggest campaign of eighteen hundred and sixty-three.

All of a sudden Howell Curtis was no longer a member of Company B, 7th Battalion, North Carolina Cavalry. Just like that, overnight, he and all sixty-three of his Clay County messmates had been transformed into Company F, 65th Regiment, North Carolina Troops. And that wasn't all. Because the new regiment was the sixth from the Old North

State that happened to be a mounted outfit, now the 65th might also officially be called the 6th Regiment, North Carolina Cavalry. It was hard enough losing the name that had bound them all together for over a year. Getting two different names in return seemed especially unjust.

Nor was this the end of the indignities heaped upon the boys of the old 7th. To make up their precious new regiment, the authorities had merged the 7th with Baird's 5th Cavalry Battalion. The 5th was a notorious lot of shirkers and scrubs. Worse, its luck was bad. On a movement into Kentucky last July that was meant to relieve John Hunt Morgan's raiders near Cincinnati, the 5th had been part of a brigade commanded by a Louisiana colonel named Scott, and on the way out of Kentucky, Scott had assigned rear-guard duty to some companies of the 5th and the Yanks had given them two bad lickings at Irvine and Crab Apple, and ended up chasing them all the way to the Kentucky River. No more than fifteen of the poor devils had got out, by way of Big Creek Gap.

Of course Howell was honest enough to confess that the 7th wasn't necessarily any bunch of heroes either. Lieutenant Colonel Folk had raised it in the summer of '62, after the enactment of the Conscript Law, and most of the fellows had enrolled to escape getting drafted into the infantry. There hadn't been an occasion in the past year when more than half of them were even present for duty, much less ranging the outposts smiting the Yanks. But the ones like Howell who hadn't laid out were right good boys and meant to stick. Howell had joined up not to escape the conscript officers but because he wanted to follow his brothers Andy and Jack to war and help fend off the Yank invasion; he enrolled the minute he turned eighteen. There were enough like Howell in the battalion to give it some tone; but even so, the 7th was nothing special. Still, it had had fair luck at least, not like the wretched 5th; and the most Howell could hope was that whatever was tainting the 5th wouldn't prove catching.

Truth be told, both battalions were in poor shape from desertion and malingering and toryism. But it looked to Howell like all the horse in Buckner's corps was due for a rude straightening up. The other day, on the road between Charleston and Loudon, he'd seen for himself Brigadier General Forrest, the man Bragg had just placed in command of the cavalry. He was sitting a square, big-shouldered gray horse by the side of the road, talking to General Pegram when the battalion rode past. He had thrown one leg across the pommel of his saddle and was resting at his ease. It was a warm day and he was hatless and his blouse was off, rolled behind him on the cantle, and in his white linen collarless shirt you could see how bony and rangy he was. He had a ruddy face that twisted this way and that with quick, searching movements like the head of an eagle. His wild shock of black hair was turning gray at the roots and his eye was a wintry blue. Last summer he had killed one of his own officers by stabbing him with a pen-knife after the fellow had shot him through the body for questioning his grit; the ball was in him yet, along with the one next to his spine that he'd taken at Shiloh in single combat with a squadron of Yanks. It was his custom to shoot down any of his own soldiers he s aw running from a fight, as well as any of the enemy he might come across. Howell had heard a story telling how he'd once torn a limb off a tree and clubbed a cowardly trooper near to death with it. Consequently the boys were far more afraid of Forrest than they were of the bluebellies.

Just now, though, it was First Lieutenant Cunningham and not General Forrest that Howell had to be concerned about. Colonel Folk had detailed Company B—no, Company F it was now—to outpost duty while the two battalions were camped in a sheep pasture by the railroad near Cleveland getting themselves reorganized into a regiment. Lieutenant Cunningham was in command of Howell's picket. Cunningham was a slight, wispy, nervous man in his middle 20s who seemed never to have gotten over the shock of his transformation from a Macon County apple grower into a Confederate cavalry officer; he appeared willing enough, but he was so terrified of making a mistake that he could scarcely ever bring himself to make a decision, no matter how trivial. Behind his back the boys called him Lieutenant What To Do.

At least Howell was by himself, riding vidette at the crossing of two lanes east of the railroad, and the lieutenant was five hundred yards back, at the picket camp, which itself was half a mile east of the grand guard, where Captain Moore and the rest of the company were. On vidette duty Howell would only encounter Cunningham once that night, when the lieutenant made his rounds of the outposts. He pitied his second cousin Billy, who had been assigned as Cunningham's orderly and would have to spend the evening watching the poor fellow sweat whenever someone asked him even the simplest question. But he hadn't felt sorry enough for Billy to offer to exchange places with him.

He liked solitary duty, especially at times like this, with the sun just dropping behind the horizon and the light slanting across the country drawing long shadows out of the low places. All day the air had been red with the dust of the marching infantry and the wagon trains they dragged after them, but now at twilight, with the armies going into bivouac along the railroad, the dust was settling out and for the first time the air was clear.

From where he sat his horse at the crossroads, he could see the ramparts of the mountains in the east with the last of the sunlight on them. Just beyond those mountains was home. How far? he wondered. A hundred miles? A hundred fifty? Likely he could ride the distance in three-four days. Be home sitting in the parlor playing with his nieces and nephews, or in the kitchen eating chicken and dumplings. Romping with Bill Cartman's Newfoundland. Hunting wild turkeys in the woods. Looking for Indian arrowheads in the bottom by the river. Just two days ago the battalion had forded that very same river a few miles above the place where it joined the Tennessee, and here in the lowlands the Hiwassee was a broad and stately thing, much grander than it was in the high country at home. Howell had leaned from the saddle and cupped a handful and drunk it; it had tasted the same, like old pennies.

Junior, his bay four-year-old, shifted under him and rattled his bit-chains with a shake of his head. Maybe Junior was thinking of home too. He'd been weaned on that belly-high grass by the Hiwassee, and used to love running down the long swale below the big house towards the flat between the river and the nose of Spoon Hill. Howell wondered what home was like now. Were they all safe? He'd heard some bad stories from some of the boys who had laid out and come back. And he wondered about Andy and Jack, Andy especially, who was so frail the last time he saw him. It was clear from the movement of the armies that a battle was shaping up somewhere down in Georgia. Maybe the 39th would be ordered up from Mississippi to join Bragg. Maybe all three of the brothers would be in the fight that was coming. Maybe . . .

But he did not let himself finish that thought. He spoke to Junior and moved up the east fork of the crossroads in the fading light with his J.P. Murray carbine laid across his thighs, listening to the first of the crickets and the last of the jarflies. Bullbats were wheeling and diving overhead and he could hear an owl hooting in the nearby woods. The dusk was full of the tiny soaring flares of lightning-bugs. Now almost without realizing it, he became aware of a faint orange glow amid the trees beyond the bend in the lane. While he gazed, it wavered, nearly died, then brightened, and the unmistakable complaint of a mule came to him on the freshening breeze. Junior, who hated mules, uttered a grunt of displeasure and once more jangled his bit-chains. Now Howell spied a second glow in the trees, then a third, and concluded that a party of somebodies was in the act of pitching camp over yonder.

Three fires meant a dozen or more of them, but they weren't regular because they'd posted no picket at the bend in the road, the obvious place. Howell was acquainted with the negligent ways of bushwhackers from his early service with the 7th, chasing them up and down the coves of Johnson and Carter counties—he had even helped Colonel Folk hang a pair of them at Dugger's Ford on the Watauga river—and he was inclined to believe that the fellows kindling their supper fires over there in the trees were Yank partisans that had come down out of the mountains hoping to make contact with Rosecrans' army.

Just short of the bend, he left the road and guided Junior into the pin-oaks and found a rise crowned with spindly dogwood bushes that gave him a view of the campground. He fetched his spyglass out of his saddlebag and focused it on the clearing while Junior nibbled at the dogwood leaves. He counted fifteen around the fires, one of whom he noticed wore a yellow blouse with an officer's shoulder straps sewed on it. They'd rigged a rope corral and had their mules and horses tied up to it. One of the horses, a white mare with a spot of black on her nose, looked exactly like Kathleen, Papa's old plow-nag, and beside the corral stood a buggy that was the spitting image of Papa's, except that it was plastered all over with mud and the hood was full of holes. Howell marveled at the coincidences of war, that a horse and buggy so very like his father's could turn up together here for Howell to find in the Tennessee woods.

He eased Junior back out of the trees and rode quietly at a walk westward along the lane till he came to the picket post. Lieutenant Cunningham looked pained while Howell talked, and after Howell had finished, just stood there gaping till Howell suggested that maybe Billy Curtis ought to be sent back to the grand guard camp to tell Captain Moore. Within the hour Captain Moore was at the picket post, and Howell took him and the lieutenant and Cousin Billy out to the dogwood patch and the captain looked the bushwhackers over a while with his field glasses and said he reckoned he would pitch into them at dawn with the whole of the company.

The floor of the woods around the camp was covered with a litter of dry leaves, so there wasn't any way to flank the partisans without making a racket that would alert them. The only way to get at them with any hope of surprise was to head straight up the lane from the west. Just before sunrise, Captain Moore dismounted the company and they advanced along the road in two ragged skirmish lines. When they were still fifty yards from the camp, one of the bushwhackers must have spotted them, for somebody in the woods on the right hallooed and fired seven rounds from a repeating rifle, not hitting a soul but unleashing two or three minutes' worth of unholy pandemonium, the boys letting off a wild volley and dashing into the camp squalling the rebel yell, the partisans jumping up out of their blankets, some taking to their heels while others fetched their arms to fight, the livestock breaking out of the rope corral to run off in every direction. Howell saw the man in the yellow blouse dodge behind a blackjack oak and shoot around it with his pistol two times before starting through a sumac thicket towards the woods. Howell aimed his carbine at the man but only knocked a shower of splinters out of the oak; he saw the yellow blouse flicker among the trees and disappear.

Afterwards they counted three dead bushwhackers and four wounded, one hurt so bad that part of his lung oozed out of the hole in him and swelled up and collapsed every time he breathed. He lay there asking if anybody had seen his dog. It was a little white terrier, he said. After a while he died. Howell went over to the mud-splashed buggy that looked so much like Papa's. It had gotten turned over in the fight, and a lot of the truck the partisans had loaded in it had spilled out on the ground. There were candlesticks and silverware and chafing dishes and many books bound in leather. There were some oil paintings that had been cut out of their frames and rolled up in cylinders. Howell unrolled several and looked at them. The last one he looked at was a portrait that used to hang over the mantlepiece at home, a picture of Grandaddy Benjamin Curtis that an itinerant artist had painted on Nicks Creek in Burke County, in 1816.

Book Two

❖ ❖ ❖

The Battle

Chapter Eight

❂ ❂ ❂

In the cool gray dawn, the forty-two men of Company E, 39th North Carolina Infantry, climbed down from the burden cars, gathered in ranks on the graveled right-of-way, and stood blinking amid swirls of resinous locomotive smoke. Craning up the track along the curved line of cars, Jack Curtis read the sign on the shabby little platform by the woodshed yonder. Catoosa Station, it said. He turned to Danny Davis and handed him a dime. Danny did not see fit to smile even though he had won the bet. Silently he pocketed the coin and they both stood listening to the distant thump of artillery that could be heard over the chuffing of the locomotive.

Coming up from Mississippi, everybody had had an opinion. Jack's was that General Bragg had decided to mount another raid into Kentucky and was concentrating his army at Chattanooga. But then Jack was probably the last man in the Army of Tennessee who had that much confidence left in Bragg. The others all attributed various discreditable motives to the despised commanding general. Some figured he was on a skedaddle, others thought he was just engaging in another pointless maneuver like the one in June around Tullahoma, that wore everybody out to no purpose. Most believed he didn't have a plan at all, that the 39th was just being shuttled about because Bragg was rearranging things again, in that fussy way of his.

Only Danny Davis had foreseen a battle some place south of Chattanooga. Sure, they had all known that old Rosey Rosecrans, the commander of the Yank army, had got around Bragg's flank into Georgia. But it had been so long since Bragg had hit a lick that not even Jack had thought him capable of actually fighting a battle now. Not that Danny believed Bragg would pitch into the Yanks on purpose. "Hell," he laughed, "You watch out, Bragg will run square into Old Rosey trying to get out of his way."

Jack's opinion of Bragg was higher than most because Jack respected firmness in a general and last winter when a lot of the boys were laying out, Jack included, Bragg had issued an order declaring them all deserters. It had impressed Jack that Bragg was ready to shoot him for laying out when nobody else in the Army of Tennessee had seemed to give a damn. He reported for duty at once, but then the regiment got sent to Mississippi to serve with Joe Johnston's army. After his time under Johnston, the prospect of rejoining Bragg had doubly pleased him; as near as Jack could make out, Joe Johnston took the prize for dithering over any other general in the service.

But he wasn't pleased to hear that artillery. Firmness was all right, but Jack had got this far through the war—one month short of two years—without risking his hide in a real fuss, and he had no wish to start dodging roundshot and Minie balls at this late date. His confidence in Bragg began to wane.

Colonel Coleman came riding down the track from the direction of the station on his black stallion, with Captain Bristol and Lieutenant Grear following along behind on foot. As usual, the colonel looked very grand. He was wearing a new uniform suit of butternut cloth that set off to advantage the stars on his collar and the gold braid chicken-guts on his sleeves. The captain and the lieutenant were both Georgia farmers and looked it, next to the colonel who had once run against Zeb Vance for governor and was a distinguished Buncombe County lawyer before the war and always carried himself as if he was on his way to court to plead a case of great importance.

Just in front of Jack and Danny, the colonel drew rein and exchanged salutes with Bristol and Grear. "Gentlemen," he said in his resonant voice, "today the 39th has the right of the brigade. I expect your smartest marching and, mind you, no straggling." Jack and Danny rolled their eyes at each other. Having the right of the brigade meant that the 39th would be at the head of the column, the first to deploy when they struck the Yanks. "Bet you another dime," said Jack. "Bet you when the shooting starts, I run like hell." That did make Danny smile. "Taken," he said.

The weather was good for marching, brisk and cloudy, with a morning mist clinging to the low places. Contrary to Colonel Coleman's instructions, the 39th marched the way it always did, which was the same way every outfit in the Confederate States Army marched, in a weaving, winding, head-bobbing mob, scattering hosts of stragglers on all sides as the boys spied a wellhouse where they could fetch a drink or an orchard where they could pick apples or a pigpen where they could steal a shoat for supper. Despite his earlier admonition, the colonel didn't seem to care. Once they got started he never looked back. He was riding with General

McNair and General Gregg and General Bushrod Johnson, and in the manner of high officers they were too intent on basking in their own splendor to care about the decorum of the march.

Just beyond Catoosa Station, three more brigades were waiting in column on either side of the road. They were mostly dressed in homespun and had a hard look about them. About half of them were barefoot and a few had pairs of shoes tied to the ends of their muskets, saving them for a hard march. Others were carrying skillets stuck down their musket barrels and part of a ham was spiked on one fellow's bayonet. They smelled to high heaven. Their colors were cased, so some of the boys hollered at them asking where they were from. Texas and Tennessee, they replied. One brigade of Tennesseans was General Johnson's, but on account of him having command of the division, they were under their senior colonel, named Fulton. The other belonged to General Gregg. The Texans were commanded by a General Robertson whom they called Old Polly. Once the way was clear, they commenced filing into the road and joined the column. Some regiment back there had a party of musicians, and they struck up Jefferson and Liberty on the fifes and drums, and for a while everybody who could hear actually marched in step.

The column had gone about three miles along the rutted, red-dirt lane with the railroad line on the right and shaggy cotton fields on the left, when an officer nobody knew came pounding up from the rear on a chestnut horse covered with sweat-foam. A halt was called while he spoke to General Johnson with an air of urgency. Jack saw him point back the way they had come. General Johnson swore. Danny remarked, "We ain't been on the ground an hour and already the orders has been changed." William Crisp, who was next to

Jack, said, "Likely they'll load us on the cars now and ship us back to Mississippi."

But they didn't. It was only a short countermarch, which was vexing but had the considerable advantage in Jack's mind of transforming the head of the column into the tail. Now the 39th would travel in comparative safety at the hind end of the division. Let General Johnson's Tennesseans and the Texans and those Arkansas boys who made up the rest of the brigade face the Yankees first. Jack's spirits picked up. As they trudged south again through the lifting fog, the artillery firing to the west died away and they marched along in an ominous silence broken only by the rattle of their equipment and the plagues of coughing that periodically swept the column on account of the road-dust their tramping stirred up.

At the little hamlet of Ringgold Station on the railroad, which they'd passed not thirty minutes before as they headed north, they now took a fork to the right but stopped again when a courier rode in. Presumably this meant new orders for General Johnson, though being at the rear of the column, Jack could now see nothing of the headquarters goings-on. He and Danny and William Crisp grounded their muskets and lit up their pipes and smoked, leaning on their Enfields. For William's benefit, Jack pointed out that they had turned west and weren't going back to Mississippi after all. "But we *are* headed towards the place all them big guns were a-shooting," William bleakly replied.

William and Danny fell to cursing General Bragg for the fix it looked like they were getting into. What Jack had once admired in Bragg, they condemned as the petty, bullying tyrannies of a drillmaster promoted beyond his capacity. "He's a great one for shooting his own poor soldiers for desertion," William declared, "but he don't seem to care much for killing Yanks. This here fight, if we have one, is a pure axy-dent."

Danny concurred. "I reckon," said he, "Bragg's the yellowest general we got."

Jack kept silent, though he disagreed. Joe Johnston, his own private candidate for the yellowest of army commanders, was inexplicably popular in the ranks and Jack had learned not to run him down in front of the boys. The difference, he guessed, was that Joe Johnston knew how to ingratiate himself with the troops by showing he thought them too precious to risk in battle. Bragg, on the other hand, never concealed the fact he considered a soldier's life cheap as dirt.

Furthermore, nobody could think of a battle Joe Johnston had ever fought, at least not since coming West, and, partly because he wouldn't square off with Grant, Vicksburg had fallen to the Yanks. At least Bragg had fought Perryville and Murfreesboro and was getting ready to fight this one. It was true that when he did fight he generally got whipped, but it didn't seem to Jack that he was as much afraid of a scrap as the boys said.

Presently the column shuffled into motion again, and word filtered along the files that somebody had spied Yankee cavalry up front.

In ten minutes another halt was called. Jack could see the ragged top of a ridge up ahead, but he could see no Federal horsemen. Buzzards were circling lazily over the ridge. Closer to, next to a little creek, there was an old clapboard grist mill with a foundation of reddish rock bound with white mortar. Its wheel turned slowly, making a drowsy sound. The noise comforted him. He thought about the mill on Downings Creek near home. For some reason he remembered the vivid green of the moss on its wheel, and how the water in the millpond smelled a little of mint. A spatter of carbine fire in the distance, over towards the ridge, shortened his breath. He thought about having a smoke, but knew if he tried to light his pipe his hands would shake and Danny and William would see. Soon the shooting ended and it was quiet again for twenty more minutes. They waited in the road, four abreast with their muskets at right-shoulder shift, listening to the turning of the mill-wheel.

The next thing he knew, all the officers were bawling commands. The drums began to beat. William and Danny and the rest of the platoon turned right and Jack followed as best he could. The orders had caught him daydreaming and he did not know what they had been. He did not realize that the regiment was standing in line of battle till he noticed the expanse of distance in front of him and then glanced left past H Company and saw the color guard on the C Company front uncase the blood-red flag with its blue St. Andrew's cross sewn with white stars, with the lettering on it that said PERRYVILLE and MURFREESBOROUGH. He looked around in shock. Fulton's and Gregg's boys were forming on the right, their double lines unwinding in front of the mill. Once in place, they stripped off their blanket rolls and began taking the skillets and hams and brogans off the ends of their muskets. Directly ahead, the Arkansas regiments were making up the first line of his own brigade. Beyond them, a scatter of skirmishers was advancing up the grassy slope of the ridge. General McNair, on his dappled horse, rode back and forth along the brigade front, thoughtfully stroking his beard.

The skirmishers went into the trees and over the ridge and pretty soon you could hear the faint popping of their muskets on the other side. General McNair pulled his sword and waved it in the air and the first line advanced, the Arkansas boys touching elbows, their musket-barrels slanting every which way. Crooked as a ram's horn, the line started up the slope with General McNair and his staff officers riding along behind. They crested the ridge and passed over. No sooner had they disappeared than there was a crackle of musketry yonder. A section of artillery came rattling up from the rear and went between the brigades at a gallop, the gunners hanging on for dear life as the caissons bounced and jumped in the rutted road. They followed the road through a cut in the south end of the ridge and vanished. It wasn't long till you could hear them opening up on the other side in support of the Arkansans. The guns made an oddly mellow noise, wump wump wump.

Colonel Coleman rode up to the center of the regimental line on his shiny black stallion and sat peering through his field glasses, first towards the top of the ridge, then towards the cut. Presently he turned in the saddle and ran his eye sternly along the front of his line. He no longer had that air of going before the bar to argue a serious case. In fact, he looked as if he suspected the litigation might now be a poor prospect. Without realizing it, he kept sticking out his tongue and withdrawing it. William Crisp allowed as how the 39th was fixing to go in.

But nothing in war was ever what it seemed. The minutes passed and, although the firing beyond the ridge got still heavier, the rest of the division just kept waiting in line of battle. They waited a half-hour, an hour, two hours. The morning fog lifted, but presently a gray pall of powder smoke drifted over the top of the ridge to replace it, so the day remained grim and lightless. The smoke smelled unpleasantly of sulphur. Couriers and staff officers rode back and forth. General Johnson and General Gregg appeared and conferred gravely with Colonel Coleman. Still nothing happened. Jack and Danny and William, instead of being frightened for their lives, now became bored and restless, and began to complain about indecisive officers and sorry tactics.

About the middle of the morning, a little column of cavalry came up from the rear, three hundred men more or less in fours, mounted for the most part on fine blooded horses. The man leading them wore an old slouch hat and a linen duster over his uniform, with his pistol and sword belted around it. He pulled up by General Johnson and they consulted together. He had a quick, ferocious way about him and Jack noticed that his face was fiery red behind his black mustache and chin-beard. Something about him, some force, drew the eye, and every man on the field who could see was watching him. Johnny Deal, who was next to Danny Davis, passed on what was being said along the front rank: "That's General Bedford Forrest."

Everybody knew about Forrest. They watched him in awe but warily too, lest he be taken by a fit of fury and start laying about him with his sword, slaying friend and foe alike, as they had heard he was wont to do on occasion, because of his devil's temper. Forrest's escort, Johnny Deal further reported, was all that was left of General John Hunt Morgan's partisans, most of whom the Yanks had killed or captured in Ohio a while back when they stopped Morgan's raid on Cincinnati. Jack looked these famous fellows over and could distinguish nothing special about them except for their excellent mounts and their abundance of revolvers. His eye rested on a wraith of a boy sitting a bay colt at the head of the column. He recognized the horse before he did the rider. The horse was little Junior, and the rider was his brother Howell.

"Permission to leave the ranks!" he cried. "Permission to leave the ranks!" He glared about him frantically. The sergeant of his platoon could not grant him permission because the sergeant was not present—he was Jack's own brother Andy, home in Clay County on sick furlough. Henry Jackson was the corporal, and from his place on the right of the platoon he gave Jack a startled look as Jack addressed his plea to him. "Henry, Henry," Jack shouted, pointing towards the troop of cavalry, "my brother Howell's just over yonder. Permission to leave the ranks?" Uncertain whether it was seemly under the circumstances, Henry scowled. After all, Captain Bristol was in his place on the right of the front rank and Colonel Coleman was sitting his horse not twenty yards off. But after pondering the matter he nodded, and Jack handed his musket to Danny Davis and dashed between ranks into the open ground.

But in the time all this had taken, General Johnson and General Forrest had decided on a course of action, and Forrest raised a hand and spoke to his little squadron and they started off up the road towards the fighting. Jack screamed Howell's name, but the boy did not hear him. The column broke into a trot. Jack ran after it. He ran till he could run no more. Then he fell down in the road. Panting, he lay in the dirt and watched the column pass through the cut and disappear. He did not get up till another artillery section started for the front and nearly ran him over. He rose and stood aside as the two bronze twelve-pounders rattled by. The gunners jeered at him. He started slowly back to the regiment. He hardly noticed that Fulton's and Gregg's brigades were advancing. He passed through them as they started up the slope.

"Damned if I've ever seen anything like it," said Danny Davis as Jack resumed his place. "I've got a cousin in the 58th North Carolina in Preston's division but ain't set eyes on him once the whole time since the war commenced. Yet yonder was old Howell Curtis himself, not fifty paces off."

Jack took his musket back. "He looked a little peaked, I thought."

"Howell's a-riding with General Bedford Forrest," said William Crisp reverently.

Jack fell into thought while he regained his breath. He hadn't liked the slumped curve of Howell's back, his spindly neck, the way his ears stuck out. The boy must've been on short rations quite a spell to look so spare. But he'd ridden off smartly enough. And Jack did feel some pride, as well as some trepidation, to think that Howell was under the awful Forrest's command. If Howell lived, what stories he'd have to tell! Jack thought about the tales he himself could recount in after years. Between them, he and Howell could entrance little Alec and amaze little Sarah with their terrible adventures in the great war. If they lived.

He listened warily to the crackle and sputter beyond the high ground. His wife Mary Jane never wanted to hear the stories. Though he hadn't yet been exposed to the perils of battle, Jack had been in a few tight spots, in picket skirmishes and ambushes and bushwhacker scrapes. But Mary Jane didn't want to know. In her letters she begged him not to divulge any of the trials that beset him. She could not bear to think of him in so much peril, she said. He understood. But still, it made him feel peculiar to be caught up in a thing so large and strange and not be able to tell her of it. What was there to say, if he could not speak of the great matter he was a part of? So he wrote very few letters to her. He wrote Papa and Mama instead, and told them the things he could not tell Mary Jane, and asked them to give her his love and say that he was well, even if he wasn't. He understood. Mary Jane was under a good deal of strain. On account of Jack volunteering for the war, she had to leave the farm they had started near Athens over in Jackson County, Georgia, and take the children back to Carolina to live with her in-laws in a strange house full of other people's younguns. Mary Jane was high-strung and sensitive, and it was hard for her. He understood.

His thoughts returned fondly to Howell. He wondered how the war was changing him. It changed everybody some-how. It had made lazy, easygoing Andy into a worry wart afraid of his shadow, but because Captain Bristol liked him and had made him a sergeant when he enlisted, Andy im-probably wielded authority over a platoon of soldiers and, even more improbably, was something of a success at it. This was because he had been so popular for his winning ways in Clay County before the war and his neighbors, who were now the men of his platoon, seeing how unsteady he was in army guise, had resolved to protect him from himself. Cheer-fully they obeyed him on the few occasions when his orders were correct, and when he was wrong they just as cheerfully, and most respectfully, disobeyed him and did what they knew he should have told them to do. They always gave him the credit for any successful outcome. Andy didn't seem to understand that this was happening. He knew he was no good at being a sergeant and was puzzled that the things the platoon did turned out well so often despite his ignorance and indecision. He was spending the war in a fog of befuddle-ment and fear.

When Jack tried to think of what he himself had been like before the war, he could no longer remember that time clearly. He farmed, got married, made two children, lived an ordinary life. He supposed he'd been a common enough sort of a fellow, no better or worse than the next. In the army he fell into error, though. No two ways about that. He'd become something of a scamp and ne'er-do-well. He had taken up gambling and swearing, he no longer cared for the preachers and what they said about God and the Savior. Mama and Papa would be scandalized. Jack wasn't sure how this had happened, except that army life for him had consisted of little more than dreary camp routine, and in his idleness he had been tempted into sin in hopes of breaking the monotony.

But Howell. What was the war making of Howell? Jack hadn't seen him since November of '61, when he'd been a plump, rosy-cheeked sixteen-year-old, full of ginger. All the boy could think about was turning eighteen so he could enroll in the army and fight the Yanks like Jack and Andy. "Only I ain't going to slog around in the mud like you two," he boasted. "I'm going to join the cavalry and have myself a saber and a revolver and a plume in my hat, and fight in high style." Just now, sitting his horse at the head of Forrest's column, he had looked pale and wasted, barely a shadow of the lively youngster Jack recalled. A black premonition spread over Jack's mood. Maybe the pallor he saw on Howell was the seal of death, and maybe the two of them would never get the chance after all to sit by the hearth and tell little Alec and little Sarah the tales of their grand adventure.

The racket on the far side of the ridge had risen to a continuous rattle unevenly punctuated by the thumping of the artillery. "I wisht we still had us a chaplain," moaned Johnny Deal. "Remember old Reverend Talley? I wisht he hadn't gone home last winter."

William Crisp snorted. "What you want a chaplain for?"

"Why, to pray for me," Johnny Deal earnestly replied. "To ask the Almighty to look after me in the fight."

Jack said, "If I was you, I'd just send that prayer along myownself, straight to the Lord, without no go-between. I expect you'd have a better chance of getting through than if you was to depend on old Talley."

Danny Davis nodded. "Old Talley, he was a drinker on the sly. I do believe he'd lost his faith. Jack's right, take on the matter yourself."

Johnny Deal seemed unconvinced. Wistfully he asked, "Wonder whatever happened to old Talley?"

"That was a bad cough he had," said Danny Davis. "I expect he's dead of the consumption by now."

"No," said Jack, "I heard he was preaching revivals at Shook's place on Richland Creek."

Just then Colonel Coleman reappeared opposite the center of the regiment on his black horse and standing in his stirrups cried, "Battalion!" at the top of his voice. After the tedium of the last few hours, this sudden development badly startled Jack and his messmates. Colonel Coleman paused a moment while the captains of the companies repeated his command in a shouted chorus, then hollered, "Attention, by company, left wheel, march!" and each company of the 39th broke to the left into column, the guides and color guard took their places, and, at the colonel's order of, "Battalion, forward, quick time, march!" stepped off along the road towards the cut in the south end of the ridge, and the battle-noise beyond it. Colonel Coleman and Lieutenant Colonel Reynolds cantered towards the head of the column.

Danny Davis, who'd been in the fight at Murfreesboro that Jack had missed, remarked with an air of dread, "The colonel's got that look."

"What look do you mean?" Jack inquired.

"That Murfreesboro look. Like he could bite the heads off nails."

Woefully, William Crisp nodded. "We're in for it now."

Jack examined the colonel closely as he rode by, but all he noticed was a scowl that could as easily have been apprehensive as belligerent. To Jack, the colonel seemed not so much aroused as subdued, as if wrapped in thoughts that might be melancholy. Beside him, Lieutenant Colonel Reynolds was drenched in sweat in spite of the cool weather, and the yellowish-brown of his uniform coat was splotched black with it. Yet Reynolds' face was impassive behind his flowing mustache. But it struck Jack that studying the demeanor of officers was not as useful an exercise as testing the mood of one's own messmates. In the blast of the fight, he reckoned, officers were of little importance. It was what the soldiers did or didn't do that decided things. Glancing left and right, forward and back, Jack saw on the faces of his friends all the expressions that fear could make a man wear. But even though he had never been in a fracas, he knew it didn't matter that they were all afraid. What mattered was whether they would fight in spite of it.

The day dimmed, its pewter light was fringed with smoke, and of all the sounds he heard, the pounding of his own heart was the loudest; so fiercely did it beat that he half expected it to burst from his chest to lie throbbing in the dirt before him. The column hurried down the road through thickening palls of dust. Jack became aware of a line of men passing slowly along the shoulder in the opposite direction, towards the rear. They shuffled, they seemed curiously disordered, and only when half a dozen had gone by did Jack understand that they were wounded soldiers leaving the fight he was headed into. He looked consciously at the next one and was sorry he had. Something had carried away the man's lower jaw leaving only a moist red hole with a lot of broken teeth stuck in it. His tongue dangled impossibly; his face had swollen to pumpkin-size. His eyes met Jack's and communicated a sorrow beyond measure. Jack would not look at any more of these.

But soon it was hard to find a safe place to direct one's gaze. Here by the road was a floundering horse with both its front legs gone, trying again and again to rise, only to fall back each time into the ditch. It was making a sound that Jack tried not to listen to but knew he would never be able to forget. The column veered around a dead man lying in the road. He was covered with yellow dust as if he'd been rolled in cornmeal, except at his groin where a black-red stain gleamed wetly. He had bled to death from a wound to his femoral artery. He was leaking the last of a slow, dark ooze, and the pool of blood he lay in had spread around him for yards. They tried to pass him without stepping in it but most could not. Jack managed to jump over it. Further on, another boy lay curled in the ditch, his head twisted so he glared reproachfully at the passing column with his dead eyes. Only after going by and looking back, did Jack see that most of the back of his head was missing. A mule stood quietly by the road with its inward parts dangling out in loops of glistening pink and blue.

They were passing through the cut now, and somewhere ahead a regiment was firing by files, each of the spaced reports louder than the last, and the air was filled with powder smoke that stung the eyes and stank with the rotten-egg odor of sulphur. Bits of burnt cartridge paper floated in the smoke like gnats. A drum was rattling. They crossed a footbridge over a little stream. The water in the stream was so muddy it resembled creamed coffee. They marched over a rise and down a slope. Jack was dimly aware of men standing in lines of battle on either side of the road, noisily plying their ramrods. In the distance he heard the windy wail of the rebel yell soaring above the crackle of musketry. For some reason there were many pieces of paper blowing over the smoky fields. One piece struck Jack's leg and clung till he plucked it off and held it up. It was somebody's letter. Deerist Martha, it said, Lest you feere owt has hapend to mee I hassen to tell you I am fine. . . . He cast it aside feeling shameful, as if he'd been caught spying.

A small log house stood on the left of the road. It had been hit by shellfire and long pale wood splinters littered the porch along with the remnants of a rocking-chair and the shattered body of the old woman who'd been sitting in the chair when the shell hit. Pieces of her petticoats were plastered to the front of the house with gobs of gore. The splinters, lying in the dark pool of her blood, looked white as bone. Crimson trickles had run off the edges of the porch in several places. A fat black bulldog spattered with blood sat trembling by the corpse. There was another stream ahead, larger than the last one, and a narrow wooden bridge. "Watch your step!" cried Captain Bristol. "They've pulled some of the planks out of the bridge. Watch your step." The column slowed as each rank stepped gingerly over the gaps. When his own turn came, Jack looked down between the planks and glimpsed green beards of moss winding and unwinding in clear water, with a school of pearly minnows suspended above them. He wondered why this watercourse was clear when the other had been so muddy. "What the hell creek is this?" Danny Davis impatiently demanded.

"Somebody said Pea Vine Creek," replied Johnny Deal.

"Hell, no," William Crisp insisted. "I know this damn place from before the war. This here's the Chickamauga."

A short distance beyond the bridge, the column turned left down a lane leading south through dense woods. Then a shocking thing happened. It was as if by crossing the bridge they had somehow stepped miraculously out of the battle and into some undisturbed country tract far from the war; there was nobody in sight, the forest stood steeped in silence, mockingbirds sang saucily in the trees. Nervously Jack glanced about him, more alarmed by the eerie stillness than he'd been moments before by the clamor of the fight.

Shortly a jubilant commotion in the rear set the boys twisting their heads curiously this way and that, till an officer on a big roan horse came up the road from behind, drawing a wave of cheering in his wake. Jack watched him approach. He was a large man in his middle thirties, with a thick brownish-blond beard that had patches of bright gold in it. His left arm was in a black canvas sling and he was holding the reins of his horse with his teeth so he could use his good hand to brandish his hat in acknowledgement of the cheering, and as he passed, Jack noticed how white and even his teeth were, holding the reins. He wore a major general's stars and he and his staff officers were all dressed in regulation gray, something Jack had never before seen.

"Why, that's Hood," Danny Davis exclaimed in awe. "I seen an engraving of him in the Atlanta newspaper after that big fight Lee had up in Pennsylvania." They stared intently, disbelievingly, as the general rode past. His glance happened to settle on Jack; he had eyes of a resolute, steely blue, but Jack saw that his face also wore an aspect of what looked like sorrow. Jack wondered how a man so young, so heroic and so famed could have come by such a deal of woe.

"You're crazy," scoffed Johnny Deal. "Hood's in Longstreet's corps, with Lee's army in Virginia."

"They brought us up from Mississippi, didn't they?" Danny Davis reasoned. "Why couldn't they bring out Hood's division from Virginia?"

"Hood's division, hell," a soldier behind them spoke up. "Word just come up from the rear—Longstreet's here with his whole damn corps." Not even an army of angels descening from on high would have been as wonderful; with Longstreet on hand, Old Rosey was as good as whipped already. The boys vented an ear-splitting chorus of rebel yells, till Colonel Coleman doubled the column and sternly ordered them to hush. "Colonel, sir, is it true?" Danny Davis demanded, since fortune had offered him a knowledgeable source of information. "Is Longstreet's corps on the field?"

The colonel had long since grown accustomed to the boys trespassing on the supposed sanctity of his office. Crisply he nodded. "General Hood's division is on its way. The rest of the First Corps of the Army of Northern Virginia will be arriving soon by the cars at Ringgold. We are now under General Hood's command." Of course this called for more hollering, which the colonel chose not to forbid, since this time he was responsible for it.

There was no way around it, Lee's army was bathed in glory and Bragg's was sorry and second-rate. Except for that Pennsylvania fight, Lee had never been licked, while Bragg had yet to win. And here was John Bell Hood, the bravest of the brave that Lee had, riding down this country path, right past Jack Curtis and his messmates, to take command, showing them the crippled arm he got winning immortality at Gettysburg, ready to help them whip the Yanks way out here in back-of-beyond Georgia. But even as he savored Hood's presence, Jack kept remembering the grieving look he'd seen on the great man's face. Could it have been doubt?

The march resumed, stopped, began again, and once more came to a halt. Now as the afternoon waned and began to darken, musket firing broke out ahead, and the sense vanished of having walked out of the battleground and into a peaceful wood. Gregg's brigade was in front now and, judging from the sputtering sound of the musketry, he had a heavy skirmish line out and it was engaged. There was a pronounced chill in the air and all of a sudden Jack realized that night was falling. He was amazed. It seemed only a scant while ago that he had disembarked from the cars at Catoosa Station. Yet now that he knew fourteen hours or more had elapsed since then, he was so exhausted he could scarcely stand. Nor had he eaten since consuming his last stale chunk of hardtack as the train pulled into Catoosa at dawn. So famished and tired was he that his fear of death or injury—lodged all day like a lump of cold iron at the top of his chest—entirely vanished.

Now in the twilight Colonel Coleman once more put them into line of battle. Up ahead Gregg's brigade had already done the same and had gone crashing forward through the underbrush into the black tangle of the forest. The Tennesseans halted a ways out and fired a volley, which made the woods flare and flicker like heat lightning. Old Polly Robertson's Texas boys were going into line to the rear and so was Fulton's brigade on the right. It looked like something was about to commence. The 39th heard Colonel Coleman's yell, "Battalion, forward, quick time, march!" and they moved off into the dark, tripping on vines, stumbling over exposed roots, trying to dodge the trunks of the invisible trees. The leafy branch of a sapling struck Jack viciously across the face and temporarily blinded him on the right side. He blundered on, using the cuff of his jacket to scrub his streaming eye. He walked straight into a tree, fetching himself a nasty rap on the brow which caused him to lose his hat. Behind him one of the file-closers swore at him, "Goddamnit, move on, you!" He wished he hadn't lost that hat. He staggered ahead, feeling sorry for himself. All he wanted to do was eat a meal and then lie down and take a long sleep.

In the dark, the fragrance of the honeysuckle they were treading underfoot mingled unpleasantly with the odor of burnt blackpowder. They were making a terrible racket passing through the bushes and briars and dead limbs and such; Jack hoped this movement wasn't meant to be some sort of a surprise. His eye stung like blazes, he shivered in the cold, fleetingly he thought of Howell. How strange it seemed to think that Howell was somewhere close by in this deadly pitch-black night, yet still entirely beyond Jack's reach. Jack heard Danny Davis panting for breath beside him.

The woods in front lit up in one searing flash of yellow that exposed only for an instant the overarching canopy of leaves, hundreds of tree-trunks rising out of the undergrowth, and the two ranks of Gregg's battle-line advancing at trail arms, all wearing a momentary coat of gold light. A flight of Minie balls whistled past. Leaves and twigs the bullets had clipped from the boughs overhead rained softly down. Some of Gregg's men began screaming. A second time Jack found himself blinded, yet whenever he blinked, the same sight would reappear, burned into his eyeballs—the leaves, the trees, the two lines of men, all brightly gilded.

Colonel Coleman called a halt. They waited in the dark listening to Gregg's wounded crying for help, the second time today Jack had heard a sound he knew he would hear for the rest of his life. In a few minutes the order came to bivouac where they stood, but to strike no fires. Jack dropped to the ground as if poleaxed. Fumbling in his haversack he fished out the last of his rations, a greasy ball of bacon and a handful of parched corn. He fell asleep with the food still in his mouth. Later he awoke and looked up through the treetops and saw the quarter moon riding high and serene in a clear night sky. It was very cold—close to freezing, he thought; there would be a frost before morning. Autumn was in the air. Off in the woods some of the wounded were still whimpering. With their cries in his ears, he slipped back into sleep.

At dawn the acting quartermaster, Lieutenant Davidson of Company C, came up from the rear with one of the commissary wagons and they had time to draw rations and cook

a breakfast before the long roll began to beat. They assem-
bled in column on the road. The surface of the road and the
foliage of the forest were silver with frost. A white mist of fog
and smoke blurred the distances. In the chilly air their breathing formed billows of vapor. But soon the sun was up and
they could all sense the beginning of a bright fall day. Behind
them to the north, musketry broke out in a rippling crackle
and artillery fire began to thud, each report resonating in the
pit of the belly like the note of a bass drum.

Jack's right eye was swollen almost shut and watered
constantly. The sting of it irritated him nearly beyond bearing. Furthermore, he had a great knot on his forehead and a
dull headache from running into that tree in the dark. Also he
missed his hat. He'd gone back to look for it at sunup but of
course by then someone had spied it and taken it for himself.
So miserable and persecuted did Jack feel that at times he
had to bite his lip to keep from swearing out loud. Sensing his
mood, Danny Davis kept quiet, while Johnny Deal and William Crisp were crude enough to banter him about having
done more damage to himself last night than the Yanks did.
Danny's forbearance showed once again why he was Jack's
particular friend.

They moved down the road and came to the place where
Gregg's brigade had struck the Yanks the night before. The
dead had been laid in a neat row by the side of the road.
There were four of them. One had bright red hair. They were
covered with a rind of frost just like the ground and the
leaves, and it was alarming to think that they were no less
cold and inanimate. Jack saw no sign of the wounded he had
heard calling in the night. For yards around, the trunks of the
trees were splintered and pockmarked at shoulder height.

Presently they turned off the road down a byway leading through an open forest of hickory, black gum, maple

and oak, leaving behind the bristling scrub through which
they had labored in the night. As the sun climbed, the frost
burned off and they could see that yesterday's maneuvering
had covered the trees with a film of red dust which frost
crystals had mottled and spotted overnight. But now as their
own fresh dust rose, the coating was once more turning
uniformly red. In the lane the dust lay nearly ankle deep and
their brogans stirred it into dense, lingering clouds. It stung
the eyes and clogged the nostrils with grit. Gales of coughing passed up and down the column. William Crisp tied his
handkerchief over his nose and mouth; he looked like a
bandit.

The roar of the fighting was to their right now and creep-
ing nearer. Troops moved through the woods in front and on
all sides of them, but as usual it was impossible for the boys
to tell what was going on. The unit on their left was the 25th
Arkansas from their own brigade—Johnny Deal recognized
their flag—but beyond that, it was anyone's guess who the
others were.

Again the colonel ordered them into line, then told them
to lie down and take it easy for a spell. Resting on the dry
leaves and ferns of the forest floor, Jack moistened his ban-
danna with a splash of water from his canteen and alternately
nursed his eye and the lump on his head while Danny Davis
and William Crisp and Johnny Deal reposed among the roots
of a huge white oak smoking their pipes. Three artillery
pieces—two Napoleons and a twelve-pounder howitzer—
came up from behind and, with their teams groaning and
snorting, passed between the 39th and the Arkansas outfit.
They moved on and took up a position about ninety yards in
front, where the woods seemed to end in a fringe of brush.
Beyond that point the sun shone on a broad expanse of bright
field. Jack gazed at it wistfully. He reflected how strange it

was that presently men might be fighting for their lives in that pasture yonder while nature kept on with its ordinary business of sunrise and sunset and the changing of seasons, obliviously, intent only on transforming summer into autumn, autumn into winter, winter into spring.

By now the thunder of battle to the north had grown deafening. Clearly Bragg was engaging Old Rosey from right to left all along his line. So far the 39th had done little more than march around in the woods behind General Gregg's brigade and watch the Tennesseans do what little fighting had yet been done on this quarter of the field. But now it was plain to everyone that the time of the Carolina mountain boys had come at last. Jack's heart felt like it was being squeezed by a cold, powerful hand and he began to lose control of his breathing. It seemed he couldn't draw enough wind into his lungs. He thought he might faint, but the notion of passing out in front of his messmates was so horrible that it helped calm him down. He sat with his mouth open, gulping great drafts of the soiled air.

Captain Bristol walked the line, telling the boys to clean their muskets. "Make 'em clean as a whistle, boys," he said, "clean as a whistle. You can't shoot nobody with a fouled weapon, and you might even hurt yourself." Lieutenant Grear was a few steps behind the captain. "Remember to aim low, boys," he was saying. "Aim for their kneecaps and you'll take 'em in the brisket. Aim low and be steady."

"How the hell do they know what to do?" Johnny Deal impatiently wanted to know. "They ain't been in but one fight in their life."

"That Grear," remarked Johnny Deal, "is scared fit to shit."

Jack mustered enough wind to inquire: "Ain't you?"

Johnny Deal shrugged. "Hell, yes. But ain't officers supposed to set an example?"

Jack gave voice to the insight he had yesterday: "T'ain't the officers. It's what us boys do that counts." The others fell silent before his manifest wisdom. But if they had needed an example, fate promptly supplied one: General Hood arrived from the left on his roan horse, accompanied by his bevy of smart young staff officers and by General Bushrod Johnson, who in his worn butternuts looked somewhat shabby next to the fine uniforms of the Virginian army. While he conferred with Colonel Coleman, the boys drank in the splendor of Hood's presence. "It'd put fight into a plucked chicken just to look at him," Danny Deal observed. It had better, Jack reflected. Shooting broke out very near by on the left, in the direction Hood had come from. The artillery pieces up ahead began a slow fire across the clearing in front of them. Suddenly the fight was all around, and a dry fog of blackpowder smoke began mingling with the red dust haze. The sunlight dwindled, the woods took on a wan, brownish-yellow cast.

Colonel Coleman rode over to the 39th on his long-tailed black while General Hood and the others watched. "Rise up, boys," he cried, "we're going in." Jack had never in his life felt so completely without power. What was about to happen was so large that in comparison with it he barely existed at all. It was big enough that it alone mattered, while Jack was hardly even as much as a thought in his own mind. He sensed it coming towards him and it drove the light and space out of the world.

The boys raised a holler as they gained their feet, but Jack had no breath to yell. He was shaking head to foot as he stood. The colonel cantered along the line grinning confidently down at them. Apparently he was now satisfied that conditions were favorable and the case he was about to argue was a fine one after all. With his sword he pointed past the three artillery pieces towards the clearing beyond. "There's Yanks on our left engaged with General Robertson's boys and an Illinois regiment in that field yonder supporting them, and if we can break the supports, we'll pierce the center of the Federal line." Jack had heard it was customary for the colonel to make an inspiring speech just before an attack, but this time all he said was, "The 25th Arkansas goes with us. Give 'em hell, boys!"

The commands came thick and fast after that: "Battalion, attention! Right shoulder, shift! Forward"—as the captains repeated the cry, the front rank of the color guard advanced six paces to the front and shook out the folds of the battle flag and the single-star banner of the Old North State, while the right and left guides stepped up and the file-closers took their positions. Then the colonel said, "Quick time, march!" and they advanced, touching elbows now and then to preserve the alignment.

Seconds later, the Arkansas boys on the left started out with a whoop. There was no skirmish line, just the two regiments tramping off confidently into Lord knew what. Furiously, Jack rubbed his eye. It would have been a bad time to be blind on his aiming side if he had meant to shoot anybody—which he didn't—but at least he wanted to be able to see. A man ought to see his first battle. Not seeing clearly might make him unsteady, and he wanted to behave well in this fuss. He glanced left and right—Danny Davis was in a sweat but looked sound enough, Johnny Deal was taking a chaw of tobacco, William Crisp stared vacantly ahead; there was no telling how they were, or how they'd do.

The colonel was in front on his big black with his sword resting on his shoulder. The Arkansas boys caught up on the left and aligned themselves with the 39th, all their sergeants shouting, "Guide center, guide center!" Through the deepening fog of smoke, they advanced on the three-gun artillery section and now as they approached the edge of the woods they could see, beyond a shaggy hedge of wild rose bushes and poison oak, the bed of a road passing perpendicular to their march, and beyond the road a flat meadow grown thick with green grass, grass a colt would have loved to roll in. On the far edge of the meadow was a small log farmhouse with outbuildings, and west of that a field of standing corn ready for harvest, the whole of it bounded by a worm fence parts of which had been knocked down. Extending across the meadow on either side of the farmstead were two double lines of men wearing dusty blue. They bristled with muskets and bayonets on which the dull sunlight gleamed with a soft, shifting light. After nearly two years of war, Jack was looking at the first Yank battle line he had ever seen.

They passed the guns. The artillerists waved their red caps in the air and cheered them as they breasted the undergrowth, with the rose thorns tearing at their clothes, and crossed the pebbly road into the field. The lush grass smelled sweet. A covey of quail broke cover and fluttered off. Before them waves of grasshoppers rose and fell, rose and fell, as they advanced.

To the left front in a fence corner by the cornfield, Jack noticed a battery of artillery with the United States flag flying over it, and no sooner had he glimpsed it than all four of its guns spouted puffs of dingy smoke. Even before the reports reached him, the rounds of spherical case blossomed like ugly flowers just above the ground along the front of the 25th Arkansas. The burster in each shell scattered its seventy-eight musket balls in every direction. Tufts of grass were torn out of the earth in several places and Jack saw dust fly from the clothes of men in the front rank who were hit, and three or four Arkansas boys crumpled and fell.

The Yank regiment was a big one, bigger than the 39th and the Arkansas outfit put together. It stood fast on either side of the farmhouse. It was close enough now that Jack could make out individual faces. On a dun horse, an officer wearing a hat with a plume in it trotted back and forth behind the line; he had sandy muttonchop whiskers and was casually smoking a cigar. One man in the front rank, like Jack, had lost his hat; he was mostly bald and his pale dome shone so white and susceptible that Jack unaccountably felt pity for him. Behind the center of the line there was a band of musicians, five or six fellows playing brass instruments, with a real drum-major brandishing a baton. Above the noise of the fighting all around, Jack heard a few brazen notes of music.

This is it, he thought. How huge and without pity was the thing that was about to consume him. Until this moment he had feared it, but now he felt more awe than fear. He was in the presence of something far grander than himself. It seemed almost a privilege to be taken into it. He'd been caught in lightning-storms that had given him something of this same feeling. It would be the making of Jack Curtis or the end of him. In case it was to be the end of him, he besought God's forgiveness for his transgressions, for his neglect of the Christian life, for his late disrespect of preachers. He asked the blessings of Providence on Mama and Papa and Andy and Howell and all his dear sisters. He felt a strong desire to lie down in the soft, fragrant grass of this meadow. He wanted a chance to kiss Mary Jane and little Alec and little Sarah. Above all, he wanted to see the valley of the Hiwassee again. He wished for home.

Colonel Coleman veered off to the right out of the path of the regiment and took his place on the flank of the first line, and, at a distance of ninety or a hundred yards from the Yankees, he called a halt. They came to a stand calf-deep in the grass. All about them rose the lazy whirr and chirp of the meadow insects. "Load in four times!" the colonel cried, and as the captains called off the numbers, each man drew a cartridge wrapped in coarse paper from the leather box on his hip, bit off the end, poured the contents down the barrel of his Enfield, seated the charge with his ramrod, fitted a percussion cap on its nipple, cocked the hammer, and raising the musket, cradled the stock in the cup of the shoulder. "Bless God," said Danny Davis. "Fire by battalion," the colonel said. His voice had an indulgent tone, as if he were a kindly schoolmaster who wished the day's lesson need not be so trying. The color guard stepped back into the rear rank. "Battalion, ready, aim, fire!"

Jack drew his bead on a spot well above the horizon. It was not his intention to harm any mortal, no matter how blue a coat the fellow might wear. If by ill chance Jack Curtis sped to meet his Maker this day, he wanted no man's blood on his hands. His Enfield jumped and fetched him a jolt that rocked him on his heels. Poked past his ears on either side, the muskets of Moses Fullbright and Billy Garrison, standing behind him in the second rank, deafened him. In successive spurts of flame the volley coughed along the front of the regiment. A bank of gray smoke, in which random powder-grains were still igniting like fireflies, belched forth to obscure the view of the Yankee line. Bits of burning cartridge paper floated in the air. Jack gagged on the sulphur stench. He heard Colonel Coleman yell, "Load at will!"

The air nearby whickered and hummed as if bees were swarming. He glanced about but saw no bees. Then as he loaded and capped his piece, it occurred to him that it was Yankee Minie balls he was hearing; the Yanks had shot back. For a moment he was offended. He had aimed high so as to be sure to harm no one. Yet the ungracious bluebellies had fired true. Incredibly, they seemed intent on killing him, even though they did not know him at all. He was a complete stranger and had never done them an injury, yet they sought his death. He paused with his musket half-raised, dumb-struck and horrified. If only there was a way to convince them what a congenial fellow he was.

He heard a noise behind him like someone thumping a watermelon for ripeness and Moses Fullbright cried, "Lord have mercy!" and toppled forward against him and knock-ed him out of ranks. Moses' brother Miles, who was next to him in the second line, called his name in a questioning way. Jack turned to look. Moses was on his knees trying to unbut-ton his jacket but was having trouble because there was blood all over his fingers and the buttons too. Blood kept squirting out of the bottom of his throat. He said something that Jack could not hear because of the deafness. Miles knelt next to his brother to help him with his buttons. Angrily Lieutenant Grear came running over from his post among the file-closers and shrieked at Miles. Jack guessed that Grear was admon-ishing Miles for laying down his musket.

The next thing Jack knew Lieutenant Grear himself was lying flat on his back in the grass wearing a puzzled expres-sion. His forage cap had dropped off and strands of his long kinky black hair fell over his eyes. There was a grasshopper caught in his hair. Below the knee his right leg was bent to one side in a way no leg was meant to bend. He closed both hands on his knee and opened his mouth and began to squeal like a kicked dog as blood spurted out from between his fingers. The grasshopper worked free and jumped off. Jack did not know quite what to make of things. But he saw that Danny Davis and William Crisp and Johnny Deal had already fired and were reloading. He supposed he ought to do that too. He turned away from Lieutenant Grear and Moses and Miles Fullbright, towards the front. He pointed his musket up-wards at a forty-five degree angle and pulled the trigger and automatically commenced reloading. All at once his hearing came back and in the distance he heard the Yankee band playing "Listen to the Mockingbird."

Sweat was running into his swollen right eye and it stung something awful. The bitter taste of gunpowder was in his mouth and the grit of the powder-grains that had spilled out of the cartridges he had bitten crunched between his teeth. His head ached. He felt very much irked that the Yanks had not played fair with him by ignoring his good will and seeking to shoot him. Behind him Lieutenant Grear continued his hallooing and Moses Fullbright was making sounds as if he might choke. Jack capped his musket. The smoke parted for a second and he was amazed to see that the Yanks had come up quite close, only fifty or sixty yards off. The bald-headed man was nowhere to be seen. Nor was the officer on the dun horse. All Jack saw was a row of muskets leveled at him by men whose dark uniforms the dust had turned to the color of terra-cotta. In the midst of them two flags were waving, a white one with an eagle on it and Old Glory. They disappeared in a burst of smoke. A few files away on the left, Carlton Harrison fell down with a howl, and at the same time, in the rear rank Newt Robbins reeled and dropped his Enfield and started off on a wobble sideways before pitching over on his back in the grass.

Jack loaded and fired into the wall of smoke again and again, aiming high every time. Medical orderlies came with a stretcher and carried off Lieutenant Grear and Moses Fullbright. The Yankee battery by the cornfield dropped in some more rounds of spherical case, and one explosion brought down Zeke Sexton and Marcus Magaha both. Zeke lay trembling as if he'd taken a palsy, but the Magaha boy fell and did not move afterwards. Presently, Jack noticed with a shock that Colonel Coleman had taken such permanent leave of his dignity as to dismount from his stallion and get down on the ground on all fours. Jack stared as the colonel craned his head to peer underneath the hovering pall of smoke. Only then did Jack understand that he meant to spy out the condition of the Yankee line. Soon he sprang to his feet and took off his hat and stuck it on the point of his sword. Coming to the right flank, he stood between ranks and yelled at them over the crack and rattle of the fight: "All right, boys, they're looking mighty shaky over yonder. So we're going to charge 'em. We'll hit 'em at the double-quick and they'll run, I promise you!" His smile was broad and confiding in his gray-shot beard. "What do you say, boys?" They cheered just as he had expected, but their tongues were so swollen and their throats so parched from biting cartridges that the sound they made was more of a croak than a cheer.

The colonel didn't seem to mind. He was under Hood's eye and Bushrod Johnson's. He remounted his black and waved his hat in a circle high over his head and gave the orders to fix bayonets and charge. They twisted the bayonets onto the snouts of their Enfields and started forward through the stinking smoke with the Minie balls making sounds like ripping cloth around them. The rebel yell started, faint at first because of their burnt-out voice boxes, but as they broke into the sunlight and saw the Yankee line weaving not twenty yards in front, the thin cry became a scream that soared above the crash of the musketry. The Yanks fired one more volley before they ran. They killed poor Henry Jackson, the corporal who had grudgingly allowed Jack to leave the ranks and chase after Howell, and they killed Hiram Stephenson, a Macon County boy of only seventeen years, whose papa raised hogs on Burningtown Creek.

And they hit Jack Curtis in the top of his right shoulder and broke his collarbone. But the ball passed on through

without doing any more damage. It was a thirty-day furlough wound for sure. Jack lay on his back in the long grass
and gazed up at the blue sky, till Danny Davis bent over him
with a grin and said, "You owe me a dime."

Book Three

● ● ●

The Return

Chapter Nine

❖ ❖ ❖

1

Bridgeman withdrew up the Ocoee and hid out on Frog Mountain. The first day or so he was in a hopeful mood in spite of what had happened to him at Cleveland. He reasoned that if the whole Rebel army was headed south into Georgia after Rosecrans, then he could lay low till the tail of it passed him by. Then he could safely move up to General Burnside at Knoxville. Or it might be that Burnside would be coming down from there himself, following on the heels of the Rebels, and Bridgeman could meet him on the road.

Either way, Bridgeman believed he could have an interview with Burnside and show how he had succeeded where Goldman Bryson had failed in the business of supporting loyalism and meting out punishment to the secesh in the North Carolina high country. Admittedly Bridgeman had only six of the Yellow Jackets left. But that was six more than had returned from Bryson's expedition. Surely this was evidence of Bridgeman's superior skill and heroism. He thought he could convince Burnside to reward him with a regular commission now.

At first he thought of taking his next raid into Madison, Yancey or Mitchell, in hopes that district hadn't been picked over as bad as Clay and Cherokee, and because the Thomas Legion generally didn't patrol that far east. But then, the more he pondered it, the worse he wanted to go back into Clay. There was still the Quillen treasure he had missed. And there was also the matter of old Judge Curtis, which had come to be like a bone stuck crosswise in his throat.

Ever since leaving the Judge's place unburnt, Bridgeman had had the feeling he was jinxed. No sooner had he showed clemency to Old Man Curtis than a spate of evil luck had befallen the Yellow Jackets—first the Puckett ambush, next the Quillens making off with their cache of goods, then in quick succession the attacks by the Qualla redskins, Vaughn's cavalry, and now these Rebs at Cleveland. Bridgeman came to believe he'd made a mistake at Curtis's. He thought he should go back and rectify it, else his run of bad fortune might continue. It was true that the old fellow had once done him a kindly turn, but that was a long time ago and Bridgeman had paid him back by leaving his fine home untouched and allowing himself to be deflected off to the Pucketts and the Quillens. He and the judge were quits now. And he had given Curtis fair warning that if he came through the Hiwassee valley again, things would be different. He could burn the old aristocrat out with a clear conscience next time.

But by the third day after Cleveland, Bridgeman had come down with a bad cold and sore throat, and the sicker he got, the more his spirits sank. Now it seemed to him that he had failed so badly that Burnside would laugh him out of camp. He had left Cosby with fifty men, and now all but half a dozen were gone. He had collected the riches of four counties, only to lose everything but three thousand dollars in specie and some odds and ends of jewelry and plate. He lay coughing and sniffling in his blankets in the little cabin they found at the head of a creek and told himself he was a figure of ridicule for the mess he had made of things.

The six who were with him felt themselves released from their obligation when they saw Bridgeman take to his bed. The night of the third day they stole out of the cabin, taking the goods with them, and rode down the creek to Towee Falls and next day headed north towards Tellico Plains. They took Bridgeman's horse too, so he wouldn't be able to follow.

Awakening to find the six gone, with all that remained of the treasure, was enough to remedy Bridgeman's despondency and his sickness both. He trailed them on foot to the falls and at a farmstead below the falls he stole a mule and then made better time. All that day and the next, he followed them north and east through the foothills, and the evening of the second day he crossed the river above Tellico Plains and at Poplar Spring turned up along the east side of Little Mountain.

There was a line of hills between this region and the flat country to the west where Rosecrans and Bragg had maneuvered on their way down into Georgia, so the armies hadn't troubled the district at all. It was a place of slender valleys nestled between low ranges, and in the cool, overcast weather the green of it looked especially vivid. The harvest had commenced on the small farms perched on the hillsides and wedged into the narrow bottoms. The people he spoke to were congenial, and when he explained that his friends were expecting him to catch up to them after a visit he had made to an aunt who lived down by Nine Mile Creek above Old Fort Loudon, they were eager to tell him which way the six had gone. Midmorning of the following day, he was heading up the steep-sided valley between the Black Sulphur Knobs and Chilhowee Mountain when he saw them ahead of him, riding single-file along the sunken road between two zig-zags of rail fence. He followed at a distance till nightfall, hanging back so they wouldn't spy him.

He needn't have been so careful. They were paying no mind to anything and in fact seemed to be drunk. Now and then they would howl and scream and fire off their pistols. They sang a number of songs. When they made camp by a little stream to the left of the road, they set no guard. Bridgeman turned the mule loose and waited in a copse of trees a half-mile away till the moon was high. It was a quarter moon, thin as a fingernail-paring. Under its pale light, he crept along the fence line to the place where there was a break in the fence. They were camped at a spot where the neighborhood folk had made a little picnic ground by the stream. There was a trestle table with benches and a stone hearth with a gridiron for cooking. The one called Poison Ivy was stretched out asleep on the table. The rest lay snoring around the hearth, where the embers of their fire still glowed. They stank of sourmash.

Bridgeman started with Poison Ivy, who was the most convenient on account of lying on the table and was also most likely the leader. Bridgeman closed a hand over his mouth and cut his throat with one curling motion of his bowie knife. Then as Poison Ivy commenced to wallow he stuck the knife in his heart and drew it quickly out. Bridgeman had to hold him awhile till he quit struggling. But except for some gurgling he died so quietly that no one stirred. Bridgeman served the others just the same, except for young Wally Parsons who he thought might be edified to awaken in the morning surrounded by his butchered messmates. He rigged a lead-rope for the horses and loaded them with the saddlebags containing the money and the burlap sacks full of treasure, and mounting his own horse, he started off along the line of Chilhowee towards Cosby.

At daybreak he shot a rabbit and stopped to eat it for breakfast. While he ate, it occurred to him that by recovering his goods he might have begun the reversal of his run of bad luck. Overnight his confidence had returned and he noticed that even his cold and sore throat had disappeared. He examined his prospects in a new light. All of a sudden it made no sense at all to go begging to Burnside for authority to fit out another command. He need not bother with authority of any kind—not even the pretense of authority he had used to organize the Yellow Jackets around Cosby to begin with. His own personal authority was enough. The hills on the Tennessee-Carolina border were full of the sort of men he required, desperate men who would take desperate chances. All he need do was send out the word.

This time, though, he would take a smaller band. Ten or twelve at the most. Picked men he could count on. No more Bloody Bobs or Poison Ivys or Wally Parsonses to funk out and turn on him. Men of character. He resumed his journey in high spirits. His mind was busy laying plans as he rode leading the five horses. That evening as he struck his fire, he thought he heard the faint rumble of artillery, far away to the south.

2

Howell had suffered such torments of dread and worry since discovering the portrait of Grandaddy Curtis amid the plunder at the bushwhacker camp that he had passed through the entire battle of Chickamauga in a kind of daze. After the fighting ended on the evening of the third day, General

Forrest led the cavalry out to worry the rear of Old Rosey's army as it retreated towards Chattanooga. It was then that Howell realized he had no clear recollection of the scrap he had just come through. Yet the fears that plagued him were so vivid they seemed like memories of things he had actually witnessed and not just imagined. What was in his mind had become more real than his own experience.

He saw the manse ablaze on its hilltop above the river. He saw Papa hanged from the stoutest limb of the big Spanish oak in the side yard—he knew the very bough, he knew just how slowly and irrevocably Papa's body had rotated at the rope's end. He saw Andy dragged outside from his sickbed and shot to pieces on the ground while poor Mama and Salina stood watching. He saw his little sisters and the Cartman boys cringing in terror. He saw Betty, in high temper, try to fight them. He saw them strike her down, saw them . . .

He had questioned the three wounded partisans, but of course they swore they knew nothing of the portrait. They had never been in Carolina at all, much less up the Hiwassee as far as the Nantahalas. Howell had wanted to make them tell, but Captain Moore stopped him. It even became necessary for Captain Moore to put him under guard till the provost troops came to take the prisoners off. The most Howell could do was write a letter home, hoping that whoever had survived would get it. He wrote of finding the picture. He said he prayed they were not hurt as badly as his imagination told him they were. He said he was in good health, but now that renegades had befouled his home he was thinking of deserting because what remained of his family needed someone to protect them.

He had carried the rolled-up painting of Grandaddy Curtis in his saddlebag all through the battle. Of the three days' bitter fighting in the woods and thickets along the

Chickamauga, one moment only could he recall. There had been a time on the first day of the fight when he had thought Jack was near. General Pegram had sent him up the Chickamauga to deliver a dispatch to General Forrest, who was on the right flank of the army helping four infantry brigades under General Bushrod Johnson force a crossing to try and get into the Yankee rear. A colonel named Rambaut took the message and ordered Howell to stay at headquarters in case Forrest needed word sent back to Pegram. While he waited, he felt Jack's presence, and as the column got under way, somehow the exact sound of Jack's voice seemed to ring in his ear. It had troubled him.

But all the rest was a blur. He spent most of the battle following the general, who rode everywhere at a wild dash, across the creek, up and down the country lanes, through woods and thickets and briar patches, cursing like a devil, stopping only to bawl orders or, more often, to get down on the ground with his dismounted troopers and shoot at the Yanks with his pair of navies. Howell became accustomed to the sight of Forrest's oily black curls lying on the sweaty nape of his neck because this was the view he most often had, riding immediately behind him. It was curious that of all the exciting events that must have befallen him, the sight of the hair coiled on his commander's sunburned neck was all he would carry away from the great battle.

After the Chickamauga fight, the 65th North Carolina took up picket duty above Chattanooga. While on picket, Howell thought more and more about leaving the army and going home. He knew there could be no answer to his letter even if someone there had written him; the mails almost never caught up with the fast-moving cavalry. But before he could make up his mind to desert, the 65th was ordered up to Harrison to counter a Yankee force said to be approaching from the direction of Knoxville. On the way, they were diverted to Charleston, where under General Forrest's eye they fought a short action with some Federal horse and drove it back on its supports, chasing the Yanks as far as the little hamlet of Philadelphia. Then they retreated, first to Charleston and then to the Sweetwater Valley. Going and coming on this march, they forded the Hiwassee River, and when he once again tasted the old-pennies flavor of its waters, the pull of home grew so strong that Howell found himself weeping.

Soon after this, General Forrest was transferred to another command. The boys were not sorry to see him go: he had worked them mighty hard and exposed them to much more danger than they were used to. Still, for a time they had shared some of his fame and that had made them feel special. Now they lapsed into what they had been before General Forrest arrived—just another nearly used-up cavalry outfit, half of whom were looking for a way to skip out. At the end of October the mounted troops in Bragg's army were reorganized. This was the second reorganization in as many months and made the boys of Colonel Folk's old 7th—who were still getting over the ignominy of being merged with Baird's luckless 5th Battalion—groan and grumble anew. The 65th ended up under General "Fighting Joe" Wheeler's command, in Tom Harrison's brigade of Wharton's division.

General Wheeler was a sawed-off little cuss with an unfortunate habit of wearing long frock uniform coats a size or two too large for him. He looked like a boy dressing up in his papa's clothes, except for his ferocious black beard. As his nickname implied, he enjoyed a fight. But he lacked General Forrest's terrible determination. Most anything Wheeler started would pretty soon peter out, whereas Forrest would go the whole distance even if it killed him and you both. There were rumors the two hated each other so much they refused to serve together ever again.

Although Tom Harrison was only a colonel, General Wheeler had a habit of giving him a brigade now and then without bothering to promote him. He was commander of the 8th Texas Cavalry, called Terry's Texas Rangers after a merchant who raised them down in the Lone Star State at the commencement of the war and then got himself killed in the outfit's first fight in Kentucky in the winter of '62.

Colonel Harrison was a mean one. He had an awful temper and when he lost it you could hear his hectoring voice from one end of the camp to the other, spewing such profanities Howell blushed to hear them even after the things he had heard General Forrest say. He had a big round head like a cannonball and one jaw always had a huge quid of tobacco in it. If he yelled at you, he sprayed you with tobacco juice. Maybe he was so mean because General Wheeler wouldn't give him his brigadier's star. But Howell was beginning to suspect all Texans of having the same bullying way about them. Those 8th Texas fellows were always swaggering around camp in their sombreros and dagger-roweled Mexican spurs, drunk and swearing, trying to pick a fuss out of Colonel Folk's timid Carolina boys. In the field they were wild as Comanches and always wanted to come up close to the Yanks and fight them hand-to-hand. Howell and the rest of the 65th were scared to death of them.

Howell had begun to reflect on this. Mama and Papa had always insisted that a Christian character would carry you high in life. Forbearance, fair dealing, temperance, propriety—these were the attributes the world admired in men, and they were necessary to the winning of gain and station.

These qualities were what had made Papa revered the width and breadth of Clay County. Because he loved and respected Papa and wanted to be like him, Howell had striven all his life to cultivate the same qualities in himself. At the age of thirteen he had given his soul to Jesus. Ever since, he prayed faithfully and read his testament every evening. He neither drank nor cursed. Nor had he ever been with a woman. Moreover, he sternly resisted the lascivious thoughts that sometimes tried to insinuate themselves into his mind. Regardless of condition he judged no man, and he prided himself on his fairness.

Yet in war such discipline and such fine attainments had no place at all. In fact, they seemed to put you at a disadvantage. The ones who excelled at war were the ones with the worst character. General Forrest, Colonel Harrison, the 8th Texas boys, the bushwhackers Howell had encountered in East Tennessee. Crude, cruel men who would commit any outrage. Howell supposed it made a kind of sense. War was rough work and it took rough men to succeed at it. If you weren't rough to start with, the war would coarsen you or kill you, one or the other. Hadn't Howell himself held the rope when Colonel Folk hanged those guerrillas at Dugger's Ford? But he had been under orders, and the outliers had done murder and robbery on decent Southern men and had ravished loyal nigra women and had fairly earned their fate. Yes, he'd done a thing he could never have brought himself to do in time of peace. But under the ghastly, topsy-turvy logic of war, the act had been virtuous, not evil. Howell knew he could never descend so far as to be wanton like General Forrest and the Texans.

Thus his disadvantage. If he did not become as evil as his surroundings, how could he hope to survive? Yet to give in to evil in order to survive would be both to poison this life and spend the next deservedly in hell. The more he pondered these matters the more he wanted to desert and go home. At night by the campfire he would unroll Grandaddy Curtis's portrait and gaze at it in silent agony. His prayers did not help.

3

Early on the morning of the day after he arrived home on furlough, Jack Curtis was awakened by a mournful lowing below his bedroom window. His first thought was that a cow would remedy the one evil he hadn't been prepared to find vexing his loved ones. He knew they had been beset by thieves, crop-burners, outliers and the rest. He even knew they had been in want. But he hadn't suspected to find them in actual hunger.

Mary Jane and Alec, on either side of him in the brass bed, and baby Sarah in her crib at the foot, all woke up in the same instant. Because of his bandaged wound, Jack was slower rising than Mary Jane and Alec. He was still working at it when Mary Jane threw up the sash and she and Alec stuck their heads outside and both cried at once, "It's a cow!"

Teentsy Sarah was howling in fury at being startled so. Once on his feet, Jack hovered undecided over the crib, wanting to lift her out and give her comfort, but knowing he would never manage it with his hurt. Guiltily he left the poor mite squalling and hurried to the window. There below in the side yard stood a bewildered Jersey heifer.

In minutes she found herself surrounded by the household. There was something like reverence in the way they regarded her. She was the first live creature they had seen on the place since the Yellow Jacket raid, except for Rebecca's pet hen that she kept hidden in an upstairs wardrobe and they had all sworn not to touch no matter how their stomachs growled. Still in his tasseled nightcap and sleeping gown, Madison pronounced the cow miraculous and fell to his knees in the dewy grass and rendered a prayer of thanksgiving. Practical as always, Sarah Curtis bade Andy fetch a gun.

But Betty Cartman said to wait. "Look there, behind her ear."

Andy and Jack bent close while the cow stretched her neck and bellowed. "It's a bullet-hole, all right," said Andy. And no sooner had he spoken than the poor beast sank to her knees, rolled over with a groan, and providentially died. At once the two Cartman boys and Alec began clambering over her, assuming as boys will that she had perished solely for their amusement.

Mary Jane wondered out loud who would shoot an inoffensive cow and why. Nobody chose to say what they had all come to believe, that the times they lived in could foster anything at all. Everybody returned inside to dress while the boys capered shrieking and laughing over the fallen marvel.

At the first sound of her lowing Madison had believed God was sending him milk for the children. There had been none since August when the milch cow vanished, and while the infants Eva and Sarah were not yet weaned, the younger daughters and Jack's Alec and Betty's two boys needed milk to grow strong. These last days Madison had walked to all the adjoining farms in search of milk, but not a drop was to be had. Two days ago he had gone to Hayesville and Cousin Watson had lent him a quart, but that was drunk up by evening. Likely Uncle Amos had milk at his place but it was too far to walk.

Now there would be no milk. But tomorrow Madison would send Andy over to Uncle Amos's—the boy was strong enough now that he could stand it. Maybe by tomorrow they'd have milk. And thanks to the wonderful heifer there would surely be meat. Fresh meat for the first time in weeks. With the convalescent Jack looking on in regal idleness from a chair Andy had set out for him and Sarah supervising the work, Madison and Andy butchered and dressed the heifer while the womenfolk put up the tongue, liver, tripe and such. Jimmy and Andy Cartman and little Alec had the time of their lives wallowing in blood and hurling handsful of gore at one another. There was more merriment in the yard than Madison had heard in a month. Afterward they smoked the meat and hung it in various parts of the upstairs where only somebody could get at it who had broken in by force of arms.

4

Against the gold and Chinese red of the autumn woods at the top of the drive, a man in drab clothing sat a big sorrel horse on the edge of the road and gazed down motionless on the house. Jack Curtis, resting in the wicker rocking chair on the lower gallery with his feet propped on the railing, had been drowsing in the October sun. But now he came fully awake and began to watch the fellow, idly at first, then with sharpened interest. After a while he called, "Mama, who's that yonder?"

Sarah Curtis had been sweeping fallen leaves from the gallery floor. Now, shading her eyes against the glare, she followed the point of his finger up the slope. She studied the figure only a moment before softly exclaiming, "Well, I declare, it's Old Mose Quillen."

Jack took his feet down from the railing and stood, wincing as the familiar bolt of pain shot through the wound at the top of his shoulder. "I wonder if I shouldn't get a piece," he said. Sarah didn't answer at first, just stood watching with one hand level over her eyes and the other clutching the broomhandle. Finally she said, "Fetch the rifle." As he turned to go inside, she added, "Bring me the shotgun. And wake Andy."

After he had gone, she waited and kept watch. The man on the sorrel didn't move. She could see the animal switching its tail against the horseflies that were always so bad in the Indian summer weather. A breeze stirred and a lot of leaves blew around him in a yellow drizzle. Madison had walked into town this morning to record a deed at the courthouse and see if he could borrow Cousin Watson's horse and chaise. He wanted to carry Jack and Andy over to Murphy next week so the boys could catch the stage and go to rejoin their regiment. Things had been so quiet since the Yellow Jacket raid that it had seemed all right for him to go. And now here was Old Mose, the scoundrel.

Jack returned and handed her the shotgun. She leaned the broom against the railing and plucked off the caps and took a sewing-needle out of her lapel and ran it through each nipple to make sure the vents were clear. She asked about the load. Jack told her it was buckshot. He went to the railing and dropped a load of buck-and-ball down the muzzle of the Tennessee rifle and rammed it home. Andy came out on the gallery with the Harpers Ferry pistol. He was pale and shaken. Sarah gave him a fond and worrying look. He had got over the bloody flux, but his spirit seemed more delicate than ever. He stared at Old Mose with undisguised terror.

"I sent the others to the cellar," Jack said. Proudly she turned her eye his way. He was their paladin, tested in the fire of battle. He had spilt his life's blood in defense of his home. Twice he had even seen General John Bell Hood himself. Who could fear Old Mose Quillen, with such a prodigy as Jack at hand? Yet despite her fierce pride she still hated the times they lived in, hated her sons having to face the risk of death, brave or fearful as God had made them. The thought of poor Howell's letter came and pierced her heart again. To think of the desolate child, finding Grandfather Curtis's picture in a robbers' cache and not knowing how it had come there, not knowing yet if his family lived or died or had suffered hurt. She feared that he would desert and come home; she would have hoped it, if she were not so conscious of what duty demanded of her and of Howell.

Old Mose stirred. The sorrel started slowly down the graveled drive. The bright sun woke the rich red tones in its coat. As it descended, they could see that it was a blooded hunter, a stallion, far too grand a beast for Old Mose to have come by honestly. There was not another horse of that quality between Soco Gap and Hanging Dog, what with all the scavengers and outliers and brigands roaming the country. Old Mose himself looked a strange sight, atop such a noble mount. He slouched in his rags till he seemed to own no waist at all. His hat had holes in it and was stained an indeterminate color. He was not armed that they could see.

He walked the stallion down the drive to the cul-de-sac and drew rein as if to dismount there. But then he seemed to think better of this and spoke to the sorrel and rode up the path between the boxwoods. The hooves of the hunter clicked on the flagstones. He came past the place where the leader of the Yellow Jackets had broken down the hedge. He stopped at the foot of the steps and his smell rose and spread along the gallery. Jack looked at his clotted beard and took a step away from him and held his breath.

Old Mose nodded politely to Sarah, who stood gazing down on him with the butt of the shotgun grounded on the gallery floor and her hands crossed over the muzzles. "Afternoon, Miz Curtis, ma'am," he said in a crooning tone. Calmly she inclined her own head and wished him a good day. His colorless eyes blinked, then roamed sideways to take in the late-blooming roses by the steps. Next they lifted towards the sky, which was a deep, limpid blue with not a cloud in sight. "A lovely October day, indeed," he remarked. "There's nothing in God's creation to beat a fall day, with the air crisp and tasting of frost, and the trees in full color, and the dry leaves rustling underfoot, with that special smell they have." His voice still had that lilt. He seemed a harmless, maundering old man.

He looked affectionately at Jack, ignoring the rifle Jack held in the soldier's stance of support arms. "And here's your heroic army-boy, home on furlough, wounded in the service of his country. How are you, Master Jack? Are you healing well?"

"Why, I'm fine, Mr Quillen. I'm most mended up now. Thank you kindly for asking, sir." Jack was thinking how he had promised himself never to kill a man in battle but how quick he would kill Old Mose Quillen if he got down off that hunter and started up the steps. Mose turned his amiable regard on Andy, who stood trembling by the door. "Master Andrew, I'm pleased to see you up and about. I'd heard you come home sickly from the war and might not live. I bless God for the mercy He's shown in restoring you." Miserably, Andy spoke no word in return.

The sorrel snorted and stamped against the flies. Pleasantly Old Mose inquired the whereabouts of the good Judge Madison Curtis. "He's over to Hayesville just now," Sarah told him. It would do no good to lie. The old scamp had doubtless lain in the woods scouting the place and seen him set off.

"A pity," said Mose with a sorrowful shake of his head. "I come here today expressly to see your husband, ma'am, to thank him for the kindly turn he done me some weeks back, when he sent that fine child of Georgia, Mr Oliver Price, to warn me against the pillagers."

"Mr Curtis is a good Christian, Mr Quillen," said Sarah. "I expect any good Christian would've done the same. But I'll tell him you stopped by to pay respects."

Old Mose got a wistful light in his eye. "Respect. Yes, that's what I'm a-paying. Respect." Now he seemed to be almost amused. Again he glanced around him, at the yard, the house, the fields, the woods. He was smiling in his beard. "Why, there ain't a mortal in all of Clay and Cherokee counties that don't love and respect the good judge, and wish him well in all things. Now there's some that be as prosperous and fortunate as the judge who folks might envy or even hate for what bounty they got. But not Judge Curtis. All men know he got his high place in life by virtue. Who did he injure as he rose? None. Who did he cheat or rob or swindle? None whatever. God blessed him with success on account of he was a good and fair man."

"Thank you for the generous sentiments, sir," said Jack. In his mind he rehearsed how he would jerk the rifle to the position of present arms, cock it as it came up, and shoot Old Mose in the heart.

Old Mose shrugged. "I speak but the honest truth. The judge showed his truest colors when he sent me word of the approach of the hosts of Sennacherib." Something sly seemed to creep into his manner now; he grinned up at Jack, exposing his yellow-rooted teeth. "Me, Moses Quillen," he went on, "who others in this country have wrongfully accused of being a tory and robber, who the judge himself must've believed on the strength of these lies had done him harm."

Sarah's patience was at an end. She sensed the darkening of his manner and did not like it. "We're obliged to you for visiting," she said in a firmly dismissing voice.

But Old Mose kept on. His mood of jocular deference was changing to one of thinly veiled contempt. "Lord knows we Quillens ain't refined and privileged like the James Madison Curtises. No, ma'am, I don't give myself no airs. I know what I be and I know my lot and station in the life we had before this war commenced. But I'll tell you a thing, Miz Curtis and Master Jack and Master Andrew. This war's a leveler, that's what she is. She's a-turning the whole world over. And when the turning's finished, like the good book says, the last shall be first."

His eyes, which had looked colorless, now took on a steely cast. "When I came here today I stopped yonder in the road to admire the prospect. And a splendid prospect it is, too. Splendid and I might say conspicuous." He uttered this word with a sort of pejorative hiss. "Conspicuous, yes. Conspicuous because in all this region the only houses standing unburnt are humble dwellings like my own, which were too rude to arouse the malice of the rangers. Except for yours, of course. Your great mansion still stands on its lordly promontory, commanding its splendid prospect of the valley."

Again the hunter snorted and this time he dashed away the flies with a violent shake of his head that made his bit-chains jangle. Old Mose yielded easily to the motion of the horse and the act sent another wave of stench across the gallery. "I'm a simple and trusting soul," he said. "I ain't given to suspicion. I believe the Good Lord hates a low and suspicious nature. But I'll confess to you, suspicion is stirring in my breast. Till today I had supposed Judge Curtis suffered the depredations of the rangers the same as every other man of property. Now I see you enjoying the delights of your wealth as of old, while all your neighbors cry aloud in want. I wonder why. I wonder why the partisans spared you alone."

"You were spared, sir," Jack reminded him.

"Yes," Old Mose agreed. "I was spared. And I've given my thanks for that. But what was spared me and what was spared you ain't equal in any fashion. And I will prophesy to you—equality is on its way, my good friends. It's over yon mountain and it's on the march. And when it arrives, much as it may repel you to think on it, the Quillens and the Curtises will be leveled out. Almighty God will see to it." Then he favored them with a most mannerly tip of his shameful hat, turned the big hunter in the walkway, and rode out to the cul-de-sac. There he gave the sorrel his head and galloped up the drive in a shower of gravel and a drift of coppery leaves.

5

Madison had dusted himself off with the whisk broom before coming into the house, but now as he sat in his ladder-backed chair in the parlor with the late afternoon light from the front windows on him, they could see a faint rusty patina of road-grit on his black trousers and patent-leather shoes. Worse, there were dark wet patches of sweat-stain on the collar and under the arms of his blue osnaburg shirt. It was something of a shock to see him sitting there oblivious of even this small degree of untidiness, he who always took such pains to look his best. But the long walk to town and back had worn him out, and now there was the news of Old Mose Quillen's visit to trouble him.

Looking on, Jack thought of his father for the first time as an old man. The skin drooped under Madison's chin and had a pearly, antique tone; his fringe of hair was white, his blue eyes dull, his jaw gaunt. It made Jack angry to see how the war and all its woes had ground him down. "One thing's sure," he announced, "me and Andy ain't going back."

"That's right," Andy spoke up eagerly. If he must choose among dangers, he'd pick those at home over those on the battlefield. "We can't leave now, with that old tory around."

"What harm can he do?" Betty Cartman demanded in her feisty way. "He's nothing but an old reprobate with a lot of idiot younguns, that's taken up robbery now all the fighting men are gone." Her two boys crouched side by side on the hearth, wearing identical velveteen sailor suits that had somehow worn ragged in the same places. Together their eyes darted brightly from speaker to speaker.

"Don't forget the Mostillers, child," said Madison. A hush settled over the room while they collectively pondered the fate of Jeroboam Mostiller, who had been found hanging from an apple tree behind his burned farmhouse over by Carter's Cove last spring, with his two boys shot dead and his wife run mad. Old Mose and his clan had done that, people said.

"We don't know for sure that was the Quillens," Betty protested.

Imperially Madison raised his head. "*I* know it." That was enough even for Betty. She subsided and sat rocking in her corner. All the Curtis girls were on the floor dressing and undressing their dolls and periodically warding off Jack's Alec, who kept trying to intervene with the toy horse Jack had carved for him out of a chunk of oak. The girls played impervious to all the talk of peril. The war had hardened even them.

But Mary Jane, sitting next to him on the settee nursing little Sarah, closed her hand over Jack's on the cushion between them. In the night she had begged him not to go back. Lay out, she had pleaded, like so many others. The war's lost; soon it'll be over. Why risk your life again? You've done your part; now your woman and your children need you. But that wasn't why he thought he ought to stay. Maybe it was part of it. But mostly it was because of Old Mose Quillen. If not for that, he thought he'd be eager to take up his musket again. In a way he longed to do that.

Andy's Salina looked up impatiently from her knitting. "Well, there's surely nothing for them to rob, if they do come, except for that smoked meat we've got hanging upstairs."

"They won't be coming to rob us," Madison declared. "From what he said to Mother Curtis, it's spite and envy pushing Old Mose. He'll burn us out, is what he'll do. For the satisfaction of it. Burn us out and winter coming on." He looked older than ever as he spoke; his big hands rested on his knees with the palms turned half-up, like a supplicant's. The fury inside Jack waxed hotter at the sight. They all sat silent for a spell. They could hear Sister Martha rattling pans in the summer kitchen fixing supper. Baby Eva cooed contentedly in her crib in the downstairs bedroom.

Almost without realizing it, they had all been waiting to hear what Sarah would say. She was sitting by the window with a woven basket in her lap, darning some of Madison's old stockings. Now she became aware of the expectant stillness around her and glanced up. Watching her, Jack thought of what the rangers had done to her and how little it seemed to have affected her. She was the same now as she'd ever been. The war hadn't changed her. But it had changed how they saw her. And they were beginning to know that what they saw had been there all along; it had just taken a war to bring it out sharp enough to see.

"Well," she said quietly, "I think Mose Quillen is just an old humbug. Two years now we've been fending off Quillens and Pucketts and all grades of villains white, black and red, tory and secesh and outlier alike. And here we be still." She went back to her darning and sewed a few stitches before resuming. "Lord knows I don't fancy sending my boys off to war. But war's what we're in. And much as I favor the children of my body, I'm a proud old thing and I want to take pride in my boys. This whole wide country is a-giving up its children to fight this war. I don't see anything makes the Curtises so special they can't do as much."

She looked up again and this time she took off her spectacles and put them in the basket on her lap. Her eye fell lovingly on Andy, who she knew had dreaded most to hear what she'd just said. "If I was to lose my boys, or any one of them, I don't know as I could survive it, even with my faith in Heaven and the resurrection. But we're called upon in life. When we're called, we have to answer. Or we'll live in shame ever after." Tears came to stand in her eyes, and one spilled over and ran quickly down her cheek. Andy swallowed hard and dropped his eyes. Jack found that all his anger had gone.

Sarah turned her regard on Madison. "With the Lord's help we withstood the Yellow Jackets, so we ought to be able to withstand a smelly old gasbag like Mose Quillen. I say let the boys go, and leave every outcome in God's hands." Some of the color had returned to Madison's face; he no longer gave off that air of depletion Jack had noted. He did not see fit to speak, nor did his expression change that Jack could see. But he did run his forefinger twice under his mustache, with a sort of flourish.

6

The day before he and Andy were to leave, Jack crossed the river on the swinging bridge and hiked out to the old Indian mound where he used to look for relics in his childhood. Sitting on the grassy mound, he had a fine view of the nose of Spoon Hill with its oak trees in brilliant color, and of the broad bottomland and the hills beyond clothed all in scarlet and yellow and royal purple. It was one of those October days when the air is like polished crystal and the light glares so you can hardly stand it. He thought of Howell, who always said autumn was the grandest time of the year. Somewhere up in East Tennessee, Howell was being tormented by worries no one could ease. Those fears must be twice as hard to bear coming in the season he liked best. Mama had written him a letter but Jack knew it would likely never catch up to him. He shivered when he pondered how lonesome and scared the boy must be, and felt an even worse chill when he remembered that day at Chickamauga when he saw Howell from a distance and felt a dread premonition. Would Howell die? Had he perhaps died already, with nobody knowing? Would Jack die? Would Andy?

Poor Andy. How he dreaded going back. How thunderstruck he had been to hear Mama speak out to him in front of everyone, invoking duty and pride, Mama who knew his heart like no other and all his life had nourished his every greedy need. All that day and the next he kept to himself, not shamed or sulking or perturbed but quiet, thoughtful. They had all given him the leeway they knew he needed in order to study out the path he must take. They loved him in the special way you love someone who is helpless and innocent and too gentle for the harshness of the world. They would have kept him at home, if they could think of an honorable way to do it.

But the war was changing. Last year it was something you could lay out of, as Jack and Andy had both done, with no dishonor. But too much had happened now. Too many were hurt and dead, too much had been destroyed. If you laid out now, there were men in Clay and Cherokee whose sons had died at Chickamauga and Murfreesboro who might kill you for it to ease their pain and exact from your folk a price equal to what they had paid. Or conscript officers who would hunt you down and shoot you on the spot or send you back to your brigade where they'd shoot you for desertion. Or tories who'd hang you for a Rebel. This was why Sanders Barter and Bill Cartman lurked in the mountains and never showed their faces. As the war got worse, and more and more of the fellows laid out, they learned that home was more perilous in some ways than the army. They hid fearful in the woods, hundreds of them, with no place to lay their heads and none to comfort them in their loneliness. Andy couldn't lay out openly, as some could who lived in parts like East Tennessee, where every man was a tory. And he'd never last, hiding in the hills. He came to see it finally, regretfully. He saw not only that Mama had been right about being duty-bound, but that he didn't really have a choice at all, not now, not the way things were.

Buoyed up by his own revived faith, Jack had seen the justice in what Mama had said. If you're called, you answer. Leave the rest to Providence. Jack had honored the pledge he made on the battlefield, to renew his belief and render to preachers all respect. Every Sunday since coming home, he had gone to hear Uncle Amos proclaim the Gospel. Were Andy or Jack or Howell to perish, the family could take comfort knowing each had been in a state of grace. Were the Quillens to come raiding with Jack and Andy gone, let the Lord provide. Of course Jack feared for his beloved Mary

Jane and Alec and tiny Sarah. After the privations of a soldier's life, being with them again these last weeks had awakened all the tenderness he thought he had lost forever in camp and on the march. It was going to break his heart to leave them now. And once gone, he would dread day and night the harm that might befall them if the Quillens did come.

It was too bad Mary Jane couldn't see it Mama's way. Mary Jane had been horrified to hear what Mama said, and that night when they were alone she had uttered things about Mama so ugly Jack had insisted she must hush. But he understood. Poor Mary Jane was wearing down. He wished life could be better for her. But just now it wasn't, and she had no choice but to stand it—he wished she could be as strong as Salina. He would miss her something awful—her mildness, her sweet face, the fleshly delights she so readily offered up. And the younguns . . . It made him weep to think of leaving them.

Taking Mama's words to heart had freed him in some way. It had lifted burdens off him and left him feeling lightsome in his own skin. He could yield to that sense he had of longing to fetch his musket and take his place in the ranks. His wound had healed and the truth was, he missed his messmates almost as much as he knew he'd miss Mary Jane and the younguns once he was gone. He had gotten a letter from Danny Davis. McNair's brigade and the 39th had been returned to Joe Johnston's army down in Mississippi, and had been assigned to a division commanded by General Sam French. Danny said French was Yankee-born, but a good officer nevertheless, and the boys trusted him.

It was a disappointment to be going back to Mississippi, which to Jack was just about the most dreary and desolate spot on earth, and he definitely resented having to serve again with sorry old General Joe Johnston. But it wasn't his place to question God's will. The ways of Providence were unknowable. The notion of Divine purpose made him smile when he thought of how It had dropped Oliver Price down in the middle of the Yellow Jacket raid. A trader Papa knew in Valleytown had told Papa it was Oliver who turned the Thomas Legion on the Yellow Jackets at Murphy and broke them up. Jack wished he'd been on hand to see old Oliver. He wondered where Oliver was now. Probably over by Chattanooga, where Bragg had the Yanks bottled up. He sent up a prayer asking the Almighty to take Oliver and the 39th Georgia into his keeping.

As the light took on its evening slant, Jack stood and ran his eye again over the valley of the Hiwassee. The gold of the autumn woods took on a glow of its own, the reds turned to burgundy. At his feet the river ran clear and cool and its moist scent was in his nose and its voice spoke to his heart. He remembered how at Chickamauga he had wanted to go home. He stood listening to the sounds of the river and the birds singing in the woods and, somewhere, a dog barking that made him think of Bill Cartman's departed Newfoundland. After a while he started back towards the house through the deepening dusk. The lamps were just coming on.

Chapter Ten

❖ ❖ ❖

1

It looked for sure like Gilmer County had given up entirely on the Confederate States of America. When he rejoined Company G of the 39th Georgia Volunteer Infantry in the parole camp outside of Demopolis, Alabama, at the end of September, Oliver Price was shocked and ashamed to discover that twenty-six of the boys had failed to report for duty. That was more than half the number who had been paroled with him at Vicksburg.

Of course some of the missing had likely perished of their wounds or succumbed to disease like poor Freddy, and doubtless others still lay abed suffering some sickness or other. But it was clear from hearing the boys talk that most of those jaspers were just laying out because they figured the war was lost and there was no use exposing themselves to danger any longer in a forlorn cause.

Things were different in Rabun County, where Oliver came from. He had enrolled in the Gilmer Lions only because he happened to be down at Ellijay when the mood struck him to join up. Gilmer was right smack in the track of the war, while Rabun lay a ways off in a remote corner of the mountains. Matters were peaceful there. The armies never passed that way and the bushwhackers and outliers hadn't run it over like they had the Carolina valley where the Madison Curtises lived. Rabun was sparsely settled and many were exempt, and a lot of folk seemed indifferent to the war, except for the few whose boys had enrolled. But in Gilmer, times were hard. The Gilmer fellows, who were weary with fighting anyhow, knew their home people were suffering want, and felt their place was by their own hearths, providing for their loved ones and fending off harm.

It wasn't that Oliver couldn't sympathize with them. He could. He had laid out himself in the past. More than anything in the world he wanted to be curled up safe at home with dear Nancy and his sweet little nubbins Syl and Martha, making plans to move over the mountains to Clay County and take up a farm somewhere close by the Curtises. He was as tired as the next man of being skedaddled hither and yon by the confounded Yanks. There was no end to them. As many as you killed, a dozen more would pop up. He was sick to death of sorry generals too. Pemberton and Johnston had been poor enough. Now there was this jasper Bragg in charge of the army around Chattanooga, who everybody in the whole South loathed except for lofty old President Jeff Davis, who had convinced himself Bragg was a victim of enviers and connivers and was really a better soldier than Julius Caesar, if only folks would cease picking on him. Oliver had heard the grumbling about Bragg when he got to the railroad at Chickamauga Station. The boys hanging around the station were saying Bragg could lose battles from now to the end of time and Jeff Davis would never replace him.

No, Oliver was as out of patience as anybody. But because matters at home were peaceful, the worries weren't gnawing at his vitals the way they did the Gilmer boys. He supposed he had it easier than they did and could rally to the colors with a clearer mind. But there was something else beyond that. He was a naturally humble soul and never wanted to credit himself with any distinction. But the fact was, he had sworn his oath, and if he'd taken a lighter view of that earlier in the war, now that affairs had taken a bad turn he reckoned he must stick it out, no matter what. He knew that he might be a fool for thinking that way. Some mighty brainy fellows were laying out, after all. Hazel Cantrell was one and Lorenzo Garrett was another. Not only did they own two of the biggest farms in Gilmer County, they held the mortgages on what was left. Oliver's own messmate Billy Prather had laid out, and he was a schoolteacher and could do algebra and say poems.

Oliver had never considered himself uncommon dutiful, virtuous or even smart. He was nothing but a simple shoemaker. He hadn't even joined up at all till he learned the Conscript Law was coming. He hardly knew what the war was about anyway. He supposed a lot of it was about the nigras. But there weren't any nigras to speak of in Rabun County, and the two or three he did know lived better than he did, working for Mastin Prewett, who kept a hostel and a livery in Clayton. Most of the jaspers Oliver had known in the old Company G had resented the notion of a lot of holier-than-thou Yanks trying to tell the South what to do, and thought the invasion ought to be resisted. But it was the Conscript Law that had made them join. Nobody wanted to be drafted and hauled into the army like a collared sneak-thief. Why, the womenfolk would never look at you again.

While the old Gilmer Lions was all volunteer, the new Company G had conscripts. It was like finding termites in the ridgepole. There were only ten or twelve of them altogether—not enough to bring the outfit up to strength, but plenty sufficient to rot it out from the inside with their fear and mistakes. The boys could hardly bring themselves to speak to those poor lads. Two of them were in Oliver's platoon. One was named Bramblow and hailed from Alabama. The other was a South Carolinian called Latta.

Oliver was too soft-hearted to spurn the pair like his messmates did, or ignore their pining away so soulful and lonesome. He took them under his wing and commenced lecturing them during the next several weeks, while Stevenson's division got itself reorganized and eventually started back towards Chattanooga on the cars under the command of General Old Reliable Hardee. "If the fighting gets hot," he'd say, "don't bother using your ramrod. Dump the load down the barrel and strike the ground smartly with the butt of your musket. That'll set the charge and save you time. You can shoot twice as fast that way."

When they reached Chattanooga and got marched off into East Tennessee towards Knoxville to watch General Burnside, he advised them further. "We're on mighty short rations, so if you want to eat more than parched corn and bacon fat, take every chance you can to get food. Strip the haversacks off every dead man, Yank or Confederate. If you get the chance, steal haversacks from our cavalry and gunners too—they move faster'n you do, and can steal oftener themselves, so it's no sin. Every time you see water, fill your canteen. But look out for bad water, for it'll kill you, soon or late, and it's a disagreeable way to die."

Stevenson's division was recalled a few days later to take up a position at the north end of Missionary Ridge above

Chattanooga, and Oliver, finding to his astonishment that no one had given orders to entrench, nevertheless took it upon himself to instruct the conscripts in the art of field fortification, digging miniature trench systems in the earth with the point of his bayonet. "These here breastworks are proof against most anything, unless a shell comes right down on you. But don't think you can ever put your head up and peer under the headlog and enjoy the view. Them Yanks have got sharpshooters can take the top of your skull off at a thousand yards, a-looking through a spyglass. You spring up, take your shot, and drop back down, one-two-three, and never twice in the same spot neither."

On the twelfth of November the division received orders to move again, this time to the summit of Lookout Mountain, whose point towered over the valley where Chattanooga lay inside its silver coil of river. "Don't wash your feet till the day's tramp is over or they'll blister up and cripple you sure," Oliver told the wide-eyed pair. "And don't steal shoes lessen you can steal stockings too. It's better to go barefoot than put on shoes without stockings."

They listened so intent he might have been Moses reciting the Commandments on Sinai. It was a pity. Talking to them, he felt like he was already addressing their ghosts, so frail and temporary did they seem.

Bragg's army was still holding the lines it had held since winning the battle of Chickamauga and hustling Old Rosey back into Chattanooga. Old Rosey was gone now and General U.S. Grant had taken his place. The boys in Company G of the 39th who'd been at Vicksburg remembered Grant and didn't much like the idea of tangling with him again. This time their situations were reversed—Grant was cooped up behind entrenchments and it was the Rebels besieging him. But Grant was no Pemberton, to show the white flag because he missed his turkey dinners. Only the Vicksburg veterans felt this way, though. The rest of Bragg's army thought they were going to starve Grant out. Chattanooga sat inside its loop of the Tennessee River, with Bragg's army holding all the high ground that commanded it, from Tunnel Hill and Missionary Ridge on the right, around to Lookout Mountain on the left.

The 39th Georgia was encamped on top of the mountain amid the dilapidated buildings of a one-time resort called Summerville, where rich folks used to come before the war to bask in the sun and admire the views. The sights from up there were grand indeed. Line on line of ranges marched off in all directions. A muddy creek wound across the valley, and the little town of Chattanooga huddled in the distance with the river at its back and smoke hanging over it. So distant were the Yank fortifications that you could hardly make them out—just a pink pencil-line rimming the city.

On the right rose the naked humpback of Missionary Ridge, and beyond it Tunnel Hill, which was notable because of all the country roundabout, it was the only feature other than Lookout itself that still had timber on it, the armies having stripped the countryside for firewood. Missionary Ridge was scarred and criss-crossed with trails and wagon-roads whose red clay shone bright even in the dreary weather. But it still wasn't entrenched. The most General Bragg had ordered was the digging of a mess of rifle-pits at the base of the high ground, so the area along there looked pimpled with a rash of small red mounds. All along the line the Confederate battle flags stood out, stars and bars everywhere, except on General Cleburne's front, where the flags were blue with a great white disc in the middle.

The Yanks claimed General Stevenson had violated the Vicksburg parole by bringing his division back into service before its time. They sent formal protests through the lines, and Colonel McConnell told Captain Brown, who told Sergeant Stallings he'd heard from General Cumming that Grant had even written a complaint to Jeff Davis. Oliver didn't know what was legal in a war. In fact, it seemed odd that a war could be subject to a law of any sort. Nothing he had seen in battle looked lawful to him.

When the fight for Orchard Knob commenced on the afternoon of the twenty-third of November, the weather was cold but brilliant from a low yellow sun, more like an October evening than a day on the verge of winter. It started up around to the right in front of Missionary Ridge, where there was a brushy hill with an advanced Rebel picket post on it. The Yanks marched out in fine blue lines like for a parade and rushed the exposed position and there was a mad fight around there till dark. From the mountaintop, Oliver and his friends watched the tiny figures in blue and brown struggle in the smoke and listened to the crackle and crash of musket fire and the thumping of artillery. It was a splendid and terrible scene that reminded them of what they had experienced at Vicksburg.

After dark the 39th was ordered off Lookout and into a position at the foot of the mountain. Here some of the boys who were a lot smarter than General Bragg had dug a rude trench line some time back, but because of the recent dirty weather, the ditch was in water ankle-deep. The next day dawned cool and overcast with showers of rain. The peak of Lookout towered on their left with its point wrapped in mist. Fighting started up somewhere yonside of the mountain that morning. All day long the boys of the 39th heard the rattle and roar as it came nearer and then began to ascend the mountain till it sounded as if they were fighting near the top, among the clouds.

Around noon the Yank field guns started pounding the whole Confederate front with case and solid shot, and Bramblow and Latta lay cowering in ditch-water while Oliver gently reproved them. He pointed out it didn't matter whether you were cringing like a dog or standing on your hind legs like a man, if a shell had your name on it, you were a goner no matter what, so you might as well keep your dignity. But the two of them went on dodging and twitching nevertheless.

Presently the fighting worked its way around the point of the mountain and the boys could look up from their ditches and see the twisted blue lines of Yanks pushing the Reb defenders back along the bench below the palisades of rock that rose to the peak of Lookout. Smoke and fog wreathed the scene and the bursts of artillery fire winked red inside the clouds of vapor and powder smoke. It was something to see. By evening the fighting had mostly tailed off into scattered but continuous musket firing that made the side of the mountain flare and flicker in the drizzly dusk. The rain got heavier and there were pellets of ice in it. Captain Brown came wading down the line, passing word that the whole division would move out after dark and march out across Missionary Ridge to take a position on the right on Tunnel Hill. He said it looked like the Yanks were fixing to make a flank attack over yonder at first light tomorrow, and it would be the job of General Stevenson's boys to put a stop to that. Oliver thought it would be a good thing to get out of the flooded trenches, which stank of feces and the dead boys nobody had found yet.

In the fading light he looked over the faces of his messmates. There was Jess Elliott, whose wife was having a baby any day now; Oliver had seen a daguerrotype of her—a spindly little thing, covered all over with freckles, weary, sickly, gaunt-cheeked, with enormous eyes the artist had tinted green and a cloud of hair he'd made red. They had five younguns already, and were about to starve. Jess had shown Oliver the letters she wrote him, pleading for Jess to come home and care for her, the devil take the war. Frank Mullinax, whose two brothers had both died of camp fever in the spring of '62. Marion Simmons, with no shoes on, shivering in ditch-water. Lisha Trigg, who had the worst cough Oliver had ever heard and regularly spat up gobs of bloody tissue. Green Scoggins, burning up with fever and Jeremiah Sims whose sister had just died of typhoid and Sergeant Camp whose teeth had started to fall out from scurvy. And every one of them, Oliver included, raggedy and famished and crawling with graybacks like so many tramps and paupers. Unpaid. Unwashed. Disrespected. Commanded by a man everyone knew to be a fool.

"Fall in!" hollered Sergeant Stallings, and they did.

2

Advancing through fallen leaves down the west face of Tunnel Hill, the boys of the 39th and 56th Georgia had it in mind how slanders were circulating through the Army of Tennessee that Stevenson's division had showed yellow at Champion's Hill last May—when in fact they'd put up a right stiff fight and been skedaddled fair and square on account of General Black Jack Logan's Yanks enveloping the left of their position at the crossroads.

The slur seemed especially unjust, considering how many times the same ones spreading the libel had themselves got licked and turned tail; but fair or not, Stevenson's boys knew they bore a shameful name, and without even speaking of it among themselves, each came separately to the same conclusion while the two regiments divided around the mouth of the railroad tunnel and descended the rocky, wooded slope towards a clearing where stood a white frame farmhouse, a cluster of log outbuildings, and a row of slave cabins, with the Nashville and Chattanooga tracks running past. What they concluded was, they would comport themselves in this fuss such that no man in Bragg's army could ever again question their grit.

It helped settle their minds that they knew as well that the rest of the army disparaged them for hillbillies, crackers, tackeys and dirt-eaters, so ignorant and uncivilized as to be thought hardly fit for indoors living. Studying these matters, they forgot about being hungry, and the lads who were in faint health perked up, those whose families had pleaded with them to lie out took thought of their messmates at last, the fellows who'd lost hope in the cause caught fire again, and even the ones who'd never known why they ever enrolled, or had long since forgot why, now found reason for resolve.

In Oliver Price's 39th in particular the boys set themselves hard, because it was they who had broke first at Champion's Hill. They had been short of strength that day because of General Cumming sending Lieutenant Colonel Jackson and three of their best companies off to the east a ways to hold the Middle Road against Osterhaus. So when General Logan's people hit, the 39th was overrun. Accordingly this morning, on this raggedy hill, they had the most to prove.

Below the farm clearing they had entered, the line of the railroad bore left and headed off in the direction of Chattanooga. In front, the ground was level and open—a meadow, some fields set off by post-and-rail fences. This space was bordered on the right by a range of low timbered hills. There was a rock quarry at the edge of the hills. Coming across the open ground towards them in the bright sunlight of the new day was the double line of Federal skirmishers and behind them the Yank brigade of infantry, the sight of which had caused General Cumming to roust the 39th and the 56th out of their breastworks on the summit and send them down the nose of the hill to sieze the clearing before the Yankees did.

The artillery dug in on top behind them had been firing on those Yanks ever since they came in range, and while Oliver and his messmates sorted themselves into a line of battle with Abner Bosman tootling on his fife in the rear, they listened to the shells go whickering overhead and watched them explode hither and yon among the blue ranks. Abner Bosman was all that was left of the 39th's band of musicians. He was not a fifer at all but a drum major and his tunes sounded like it. But S.L. Cook the fifer had never reported back after Vicksburg. The Yank brigade went to ground behind the railroad embankment, but the skirmishers came on and gathered behind a fence and commenced to shoot between the rails.

General Hardee, who commanded this section, sent down a courier to tell Colonel McConnell and Lieutenant Colonel Slaughter of the 56th, to hold the farm buildings as long as they could and then burn them before retiring, so the Yanks couldn't make use of them for shelter. Colonel McConnell sent out Company G to skirmish with the bluebellies, and Oliver and his friends crept forward through the trees to the edge of the woods and then into a shallow ditch somebody had dug and started firing across the grassy open at the two scattered ranks of enemy skirmishers behind the fence.

The Yanks answered back. Just then a little fluffy gray dog appeared between the lines. It had the tongue-dangling grin that small dogs so often have. It dashed over to the Yank skirmish line and ran along its front. It would leap up against a soldier and then run another few rods before jumping up again. Oliver and the boys called to the dog and whistled for it, and pretty soon it came bounding across and did the same on their side. It jumped at Oliver and with its nose gave him a wet kiss on the mouth. Then of course the Yanks hallooed and whistled too and the dog crossed back to them.

Both sides had left off shooting in their amusement with the dog, and presently Captain Brown came along wanting to know why the skirmish fire had slacked off. Likely the same thing happened on the other side, for in a moment the Yanks commenced shooting again. One by one the boys loaded up and shot back. But the little dog kept racing up and down the lines and then back and forth between them, till it looked to Oliver like the simple-hearted little creature was trying to get them to make amends for whatever was divided them. It wasn't long till a Minie ball knocked it sprawling. But from time to time, all the rest of his life, Oliver would think about that dog.

Back of the blue skirmishers, the Yank brigade—somebody said it was Loomis's, part of Sherman's outfit—started forward in column of regiments with its left flank trailing along the base of Tunnel Hill. Behind it, Oliver could see two more brigades advancing in support. He watched the United States flag where it flew at places along the lines and he felt the odd sensation he always felt when he saw Old Glory, of sorrow and perplexity. He and the rest of Company G dropped back into the main line. Not till then did he see the Alabama conscript Bramblow lying at the edge of the woods. A lot of good Oliver's advice had done him. Latta's natural place was five spots to the left of Oliver, but when Oliver fell into ranks, Latta was next to him, turning up his tear-stained face smeared black from biting cartridges. "Well," Oliver said to him, about Bramblow, "at least he ain't ascairt no more."

"Oh, you're wrong, Mr Price," cried Latta. "I heard him speak after he'd fallen, as we dropped back. He said, 'Some of my brains are out'."

"It's all up with him, child," Oliver said. "Forget about him and look to yourself now." The Yank brigade advanced over its skirmish line and the skirmishers melted into it. The Yanks fixed bayonets and the sun glittered on the long blades in a thousand slivers of light. Still the explosions bloomed among them, fire-hearted, then fringed with sooty smoke. Now from somewhere out yonder Yank field guns opened on the farm clearing; two shells dropped through the roof of the barn in a shower of shingles and burst inside with a hollow double roar. One shell hit an old oak tree still holding its crown of dead brown leaves, and all the leaves fell off at once but one bunch at the very top. Wedged in the split trunk, the unexploded shell sizzled and smoldered and then went silent.

Presently the 39th and the 56th were shooting it out with Loomis's brigade, which had come as far as the edge of the clearing. The Georgians were dispersed all over among the farm buildings and in the woods on either side of the railroad. Oliver lay on his belly by a hog trough. Latta shivered beside him. A scrawny hen dodged by. "Catch that pullet!" Oliver thundered, and Latta gathered it in and wrung its neck and stuffed it in his haversack. Oliver nodded approval. "Now you've got the hang of it."

After awhile the two Yank supporting brigades came up and took position on either flank of Loomis's and began to work their way around the farm clearing on both sides. The 39th and the 56th withdrew, but slowly enough to demonstrate how they disregarded the six-to-one odds. They had got all the way back up the hill to the breastworks before

Colonel McConnell remembered about burning the farm buildings. Captain Milton of Company I volunteered to lead a detail of four companies back down to fire the place. He picked Company G to go. Hopefully Latta burst out, "Maybe we can bring back Mr Bramblow."

They scrambled back down to the clearing amid the shellfire and whizzing Minie balls and falling tree-boughs. They managed to set the buildings afire, but there were Yank skirmishers in the clearing now. Jess Elliott, whose freckly wife was with child and who thought his place was by her side providing for his five younguns, came around the corn-crib and found himself facing five Yanks amid the billowing smoke. He shot one and bayoneted another and knocked in the head of a third with the butt of his musket and chased the other two off into the woods. Lisha Trigg who had the consumption so bad stuck one to death with his knife. Oliver did what he must. It was ugly business they transacted, Yanks and Rebs both, there on Mr Glass's farmstead among his homely buildings as they burnt up. Before retreating, Oliver went to where Bramblow lay. Some of his brains were out indeed and he was a dead Alabamian.

They got back to the top of Tunnel Hill about noontime. Shortly after, while they were marching to a new place in the line, a Yank sniper shot Colonel McConnell in the head as he rode at the front of the column. But the boys felt they had redeemed themselves, and in spite of losing their colonel and having misgivings about Lieutenant Colonel Jackson taking command—him being a cold and prickly sort, unlike the outgoing and unceremonious Colonel McConnell—they were in a lively mood, and later in the day some of the rougher ones were even heard to be singing a naughty song.

Of course later that same afternoon, the Yankees' old General Slow-Trot Thomas attacked Missionary Ridge behind them with his Army of the Cumberland and broke Hardee's and Breckenridge's corps and routed them worse than Stevenson's boys had ever been skedaddled down in Mississippi at Champion's Hill. During the retreat to Dalton, the boys chaffed Hardee's and Breckenridge's fellows something awful, though Oliver thought it unseemly to lord it over the poor wretches so, who'd only run because they were afraid.

3

Five days before this, in a rainy drizzle near the village of Philadelphia just below Knoxville, young Howell Curtis had come to the end of his life.

Earlier in November General Longstreet's corps had marched up towards Knoxville, leaving Bragg's force laying siege to the Yanks in Chattanooga. Longstreet aimed to box in Burnside's Union army at Knoxville. General Joe Wheeler's cavalry went along, following the railroad by way of Athens and Maryville, to come up on Knoxville from the south.

For several days off and on, Wheeler's horse skirmished with squadrons of Yank cavalry and with the mounted infantry of General Wilder's famous Lightning Brigade of Indiana boys. On the evening of the twentieth, the 65th was moving in column down a country lane when a whole brigade of Yanks that had been hiding in a thick woods fired on them and then charged into their rear and stampeded them.

In this fight Howell was shot through the body. He lay on his back in the muddy ruts with the rain pelting him and a small geyser of blood spouting out of his chest every time his heart beat, but spouting smaller and slower every time. When he was a boy he had a pet lamb. It used to follow him

171

everywhere. At night he would take it to bed with him. As he lay there in the road he remembered that lamb cuddled next to him with its head on his breast, blowing its sweet breath into his nose. With his hand he softly cupped its curly head.

After the ambush, the Yankee sergeant who claimed Howell's bay colt Junior searched his saddlebags and found the rolled-up portrait of Grandaddy Curtis. He showed it to his fellows as evidence the Reb cavalry was nothing but a set of robbers, who stole family heirlooms even from their own.

4

Conditions in Clay and Cherokee worsened that winter. A band of a hundred outliers that had heretofore concealed themselves in the high tops came down bold as brass in daylight and began roaming the Hiwassee valley in search of Confederate soldiers on furlough whom they might disarm and abuse. A bushwhacker gang rode out of the Snowbirds into Murphy and sacked it. After dark the whole countryside belonged to the rampaging banditti, and every dawn revealed its smoldering farmstead, hanged corpse, or empty stable. Nightriders assassinated Lieutenant Colonel William Walker, commander of a battalion of the Thomas Legion, on his own doorstone near Murphy while he was home on sick leave. They carried off his son and would have murdered him too if he hadn't managed to escape in the dark of the winter night.

In all the mountain country, matters were the same. George Kirk and his Yankee partisans raided the annual meeting of the French Broad Baptist Association at Middle Fork Church near Mars Hill. An outlier crowd under a bandit chief named Montevrail Ray was tormenting the region around Burnsville. There was even an organized force of Yanks, the 15th Pennsylvania Cavalry, which despite its military title was nothing but a lot of scavengers and highwaymen, commanded by Colonel William Palmer, bedeviling Marshall and the valley of the Pigeon River.

On account of these distractions, Old Mose Quillen had been delayed in mounting his expedition against Judge Curtis. Complicating his affairs was the fact that his oldest boy Pharsalia had got shot in the leg by his middle boy Persepolis in a dispute over ownership of a hog, while his youngest, Pasargardae, came down with a quartain fever and lay weak as any mewling infant for the better part of a month. But towards the middle of December, Persepolis and Pasargardae were mended up sufficient to ride, and Old Mose declared it was time to pay a visit to Judge Madison Curtis and teach him and his ilk how the Day of Jubilee had arrived to wipe away all distinctions of class.

But the evening of the day before they were to go, nine horsemen came riding slowly single-file up the lane from the highroad and into the littered yard of the Quillen place on its piney mountain between Sweetwater and Peachtree. This was Bridgeman and the eight fellows he recruited around Maryville to return to Clay County and lay hands on Old Mose's treasure and then square things with Judge Curtis. They had followed the Tuckaseegee from Maryville up through the Smokies and turned off by way of the Nantahala Gorge to avoid the redskins at Quallatown. Then they had come in through Tusquittee Gap. Old Mose and his people were taking supper and had no inkling they were at risk till Bridgeman and his fellows burst in with leveled pistols. Pharsalia made as if to snatch up his own revolver to resist them and they shot him to death right there at the supper table with his mouth full of unchewed hominy while the womenfolk and younguns all ran screaming around the room.

Next Bridgeman demanded of Old Mose the whereabouts of his goods.

"What goods do you mean?" Old Mose guilelessly inquired. "Why, I'm only a poor dirt-farmer. Look about you, sir. Is this the home of a man of means?"

But Bridgeman only laughed at him. "You're a robber the same as me; I have this on the best authority."

He took up a candle spike and with it pinned Old Mose's hand to the table top and then with his knife cut off four fingers before Old Mose told. Bridgeman sent one of his people to verify the location, and when the man returned saying the treasure was indeed where Old Mose had said, they took all the male Quillens out into the dooryard. For lack of any stout tree-limbs for hanging, the Quillen place being liberally furnished only with pine trees, they were forced to shoot them.

In the pine-log shed up the mountain from the Quillens' shack, they found the goods. There was a wooden box full of pearl necklaces, brooches and pins with jewels in them, and finger rings of gold and silver. A samovar, a dozen salvers, several tea-services, and God only knew how many chalices, platters, and childern's drinking-cups, all made of silver and tarnished black as pitch. Crystal goblets with dead beetles in them and lamp chimneys full of old cobwebs. Flour sacks full of U.S. coin and greenbacks chewed to lace and rat droppings. Bone china, gold picture-frames, mirrors with the backing flaked off, books whose calfskin binding had moldered. Even an overstuffed chair that generations of mice had lived in. By the light of pine torches, they hitched up Old Mose's mules to his wagon and loaded up all the plunder that was worth taking. As they left, they purloined a ham and a quarter of mutton from the smokehouse, but nothing more because of the younguns and the womenfolk needing to eat. In addition, Bridgeman gave Old Mose's woman a ten-dollar gold piece, which she flung after him cursing when he rode out.

They set off along the Franklin road up the river towards Judge Curtis's. What they didn't know was that Captain Hines's company of MacRae's 18th Battalion of North Carolina Infantry had crossed over Chunky Gal into the valley of the Hiwassee from the east and was camped on the road in front of them. The battalion was composed of picked men and had been sworn in for temporary service by General Hoke at Morganton to try and quell the disturbances in the mountains. Captain Hines was a hard man and an experienced officer and his troops had had a wearying march and were tired of chasing bushwhackers and their temper was bad. Just the day before on Shooting Creek, they had hanged a pair of men and shot another whom they suspected but couldn't prove were outliers.

It was Bridgeman's plan to move at night so as not to arouse suspicion among the loyalists or offer temptation with the loaded Quillen wagon to some other crowd of thieves. That was why he and his boys blundered straight into Captain Hines's picket on the turnpike and were captured.

5

Madison Curtis had borrowed Uncle Amos's rockaway and little dappled horse for a trip he needed to make over to Brasstown where he heard there was a dairyman who might sell him a cow. There had been a time when Uncle Amos's place had seemed too far to walk; but these last weeks necessity had given Madison the legs for nearly any distance. If he had not hiked miles to some of the remotest farms that he knew the irregulars had spared, his household would have surely starved long since. Still, after the half-day's trek, it was a relief to rest on the rockaway's quilted leather seat and let Uncle Amos's pony do the work.

As he turned west out of Uncle Amos's lane onto the highroad, he glanced the other way, back towards the looming bulk of Chunky Gal covered white with snow, shorn of her leaves and stuck full of bare trees like so many black quills. Framed against the mountain only a hundred or so rods away, he saw a crowd of men in brownish clothes gathered on the road around a mule-drawn wagon under a large tree. Hitched to the worm fence bordering the pike were three horses wearing military saddles. Further along the pike, several threads of smoke stood up in the still air for a distance before leveling out along a single cottony line. He could make out a Confederate flag, a twist of scarlet dangling from a pole stuck in the fence.

He had gone into Uncle Amos's by the back way on foot and so had not seen the encampment earlier. It heartened him to think that the authorities may have sent soldiers into the valley to curb the depredations of the partisans and outliers. Though normally a reticent man not given to curiosity, on this occasion Madison felt constrained to investigate. Times had grown so hard it would be a boon if he could confirm the presence of the army and rush home to comfort Sarah and the others with the news.

They needed any comfort God might vouchsafe them now that He had seen fit to take Howell to His bosom. Captain Moore, who commanded Howell's company of Folk's Battalion, had written them a letter bearing the bitter news, pitiably addressed to Anyone at the Home of Madison Curtis, because of Howell's fear, never to be eased, that his loved ones might have perished or been scattered to the four winds. Madison had committed to memory some of the finest of the sentiments the captain had expressed: *Your son was an orna-ment of piety and a Lamp Unto the Feet of all who served with him, he was confident of his own Translation into Heaven and so died secure in the Certainty of Redemption.* Yet he was but a child, taken to his Maker before his time. Madison had prayed hard to grasp God's intent but had not yet found the peace that had come so soon to Sarah. Praise be to God, she said, by way of acceptance. But there was a stillness about her now that not Madison nor any other could penetrate.

He turned the rockaway in the road and drove up the pike towards the cluster of men and the wagon. As he drew nearer, he saw with a dull shock that from various parts of the big Spanish oak that overspread the road, eight dead men hung swaying by their necks, while another stood pale and disheveled in the bed of the wagon with his hands tied behind him, a noose of hemp around his neck and the rope thrown over a bough. As Madison checked the rockaway at the edge of the circle of soldiers, this man looked him in the face and uttered a dry laugh. "Why here's old Curtis," he cried. "This is justice indeed."

The remark amazed Madison, for he did not seem to know the fellow at all—although something about him did awaken a dim light in the deepest pit of memory. An officer with two gold pips on the blue collar of his uniform coat turned and asked if Madison knew this felon they had condemned to death for the high crimes of murder and robbery. Madison shook his head. "I don't think I know him. Yet . . ."

"Come now, Judge," the bound man broke in, and this time the sound of his voice called up two successive images for Madison. The first was of the leader of the Yellow Jackets and the second was of Frank Ryder whom the leader had named that day. Then a third image came. It was of Frank Ryder on the bridge at Murphy, standing by his cart among smashed watermelons, whipping a small boy with the buckle-end of his belt. He remembered the fear on the tearful, swollen face of that child. But even more than the fear he remembered the despair in the gray eyes. The despair was what made him get down from his calash and make Ryder stop. And it was what he saw in the same gray eyes looking down at him now from the bed of the wagon, despite the feigned air of vaunting indifference.

"Now you know me," the man grinned, and Madison nodded. "Yes, I know you. And I remember about Frank Ryder as well."

"Do you now?" He laughed his rasping laugh again. "And what do you think about your act of kindness that day, and the consequences it has had?"

Even while the man spoke, the captain impatiently gave a command to the soldier sitting on the wagon-box, who lashed the mules with the reins. Very slowly the wagon rolled out from under the bushwhacker. He dropped only a foot or so and then took a long time strangling and kicking at the end of the rope before he quieted. While the body swayed and pirouetted, Madison thought about that last remark. He wondered how matters might have turned out if he had stayed his hand that day on the bridge at Murphy. Then he thought about what had happened, and pondered whether any of it had been his doing. But the thing that was in his mind when he spoke next was the memory of a child's despairing face. "Captain, would you have your men cut that fellow down and put him in the rockaway? I'm obliged to bury him, I reckon."

Suspiciously the captain eyed him. "What for, may I ask?"

Madison shrugged. "We were acquainted some years ago, and I feel myself under something of an obligation."

6

He drove the rockaway down to the manse and got out to fetch his tools from the root cellar. When he returned with his shovel and pickaxe, Sarah, wearing one of his wool greatcoats, was standing by the nigh rear wheel. She had exposed the face of the hanged man by undoing the grimy blanket Captain Hines's men had wrapped him in. She was blue with cold in the raw weather and every time she breathed she blew a white plume. He could tell by her look that she recognized the man and required an explanation.

While he talked, Betty and the two Cartman boys came out of the house and down to the cul-de-sac and Jimmy and Andy got into the rockaway and sat, one in front and one in back, with the corpse lying on the floorboard between them. This was the first dead man they had ever seen and they regarded him doubtfully, as if they expected him to bound up and run off. After he finished saying what he had to say to Sarah, Madison thought about shooing the boys away. But then he figured they might as well see this too, along with all else the war had delivered to their doorstep.

Sarah pronounced herself satisfied with what Madison told her and remarked on the quirks of Providence. Then he recounted what Captain Hines had told him about one of the brigands confessing they'd made a clean sweep of the Quillens the day before. Madison had seen the Quillen goods himself, some of which he recognized as belonging to neighbors robbed out by tories months before. "We've nothing more to fear from Old Mose," said Madison.

"The Lord works in mysterious ways, His wonders to perform," quoth Sarah.

By now Martha and Jack's Mary had put on wraps and come out on the gallery with their babes, and Salina and the

179

daughters were lingering in the walkway between the box-woods at an uneasy distance. Little Alec wobbled out to the cul-de-sac and made his way to the fender of the rockaway to gaze curiously at the man who seemed to be asleep despite all the attention the grownups were lavishing on him. Betty swooped him up and carried him back to Mary.

Madison climbed into the rockaway and spoke gently to Uncle Amos's dappled horse. He drove slowly down the farm lane, with Jimmy Cartman on the padded seat beside him and Andy Cartman behind the hanged man in the back seat. Sarah had covered up the man's face again, so there was nothing for the boys to look at except his bare feet sticking out of the bottom of the blanket to show that Captain Hines's soldiers had stolen his fine cavalry boots.

There was a place on the river bank under a weeping willow that Madison thought would be fitting. The snowy peaks of the Georgia mountains were just visible over the south rim of the valley, and rising from the bottom on this side of the river were the gently rounded Tusquittee foothills, where the grass would be a vivid green when spring came. He stopped there and lifted out the body and laid it on the mat of brown winter grass while Jimmy and Andy sat watching. First he broke up the ground with the pickaxe, then he commenced shoveling out the dark clods. After a while he got warm from the exercise and took off his coat and folded it on the seat of the rockaway. He gave off steam in the cold air. Jimmy and Andy got down from the rockaway and began to help him by tossing out pebbles and chunks of earth, one on either side of him, till they got bored and wandered off and sat on the riverbank in their identical sailor suits with the velveteen worn off in the same places, and skipped stones across the surface of the Hiwassee.

None of this news came timely to the attention of Andy and Jack Curtis, who were at Brandon in Mississippi with Company E of the 39th North Carolina. The 39th was part of General Sam French's divison in an army corps commanded by General Leonidas Polk, who, in addition to being a general, was a bishop in the Episcopal Church. Danny Davis said this meant Polk could arrange to get you killed and at the same time speed you on your way to Heaven, which seemed desirably efficient to Danny.

They maneuvered to no purpose against two corps of General Sherman's Yanks around Jackson for awhile in February, then got sent first to Mobile and then—when the Federals failed to attack there—on to the Yellow River by Pensacola Bay in Florida, where the Yanks were supposed to strike next but didn't. There they had an easy duty in the balmy weather and devoted themselves to camp life and hunting and fishing. The only blot on this time was their knowledge that poor Howell had gone to his reward. Howell's passing hadn't struck Jack as a dread surprise but instead had only confirmed what he felt when he glimpsed the boy at Chickamauga. It almost made him feel complicit in the death to think that maybe he foresaw it. He tried taking refuge in his faith, but found it to be waning again amid the temptations of the camp. He reckoned he was just a lost soul no matter what.

It was in camp on the Yellow River that Mama's letter reached them telling of the strange entwined fates of Old Mose Quillen and the leader of the Yellow Jackets. But they had scant time to marvel at that odd conjunction of events, on account of General Polk receiving orders to carry his corps into northwest Georgia, where the Army of Tennessee was dug in to resist a drive on Atlanta by a force of seven Union army corps commanded by their old antagonist General Sherman. General Bragg had been dismissed for losing the battles around Chattanooga and Old Joe Johnston now commanded the Army of Tennessee in his stead. Jack, who once admired Bragg and detested Johnston, heard this unmoved. Bragg had won Chickamauga but had ended up losing it by not crushing Old Rosey and letting him run off to Chattanooga. One general or another, Jack had learned that they were all the same.

The 39th force-marched to Pollard, Alabama, from whence the boys were transported by rail in burden cars to Resaca. They arrived on the twelfth of May, a Thursday, and took position on the far left flank of Johnston's army, behind breastworks on fortified high ground overlooking the drainage of Camp Creek, a stream that wound along the whole front of Polk's corps. A ways to the south, at the very end of the line, the creek joined the Oostanaula River, which could be seen flowing past through a flat valley on the left, glinting in the sun like a strip of wrinkled gold foil.

Directly in front, beyond Camp Creek, stood a row of three hills, the ones on either end thickly wooded and the one in the middle bald. On these hills and behind them were the Yankee lines. The boys of the 39th were able to make these observations in the failing light of evening as they filed into the ditches along a crest above the village of Resaca with the line of the Western & Atlantic Railroad to their rear. Their brigade, which had been General McNair's and then Colonel Coleman's when McNair was wounded at Chickamauga, was now commanded by General Dan Reynolds, an Arkansas lawyer who Danny Davis observed had the biggest and shaggiest goatee in the service, big enough for birds to nest in. General Cantey was their division commander.

That night Oliver Price sauntered in to visit. Having heard that Polk's corps had arrived from Mississippi, he wheedled a pass out of his captain and walked the whole four-and-a-half miles of the line from where Stevenson's divison was, away over on the far right, asking for the 39th North Carolina at every post he came to. They had a lively reunion in a traverse behind the main ditch, with a little pit-fire going. Jack and Andy introduced Oliver to Danny Davis, William Crisp and Johnny Deal, and recounted for them how Oliver had discomfited the Yellow Jackets last fall at Murphy. Next they told Oliver the curious tale of how the Quillens and the leader of the bushwhackers had perished, and related the death of Howell, for which Oliver expressed himself powerful sad.

As much of a delight as it was having Oliver drop in, Jack felt poorly that night, and after a couple of hours' conversation excused himself and turned in. For days he had been suffering what he thought was a bad cold and now he was feeling feverish. He rolled up shivering in his blanket. His last wakeful sights and sounds were of Oliver telling about the Chattanooga fight in his large voice, with his small shoemaker's hands gesturing fluently in the firelight.

At daylight Jack awoke on fire with fever and coughing up gobs of phlegm, but when the long roll began to beat, he had no choice but to take up his musket. General Reynolds ordered the whole of the 39th out as skirmishers, and when the boys scrambled down the red-dirt slope of the breastworks among the abatis and cheveaux-de-fris, Andy had to prop Jack up by winding an arm under his armpits. Jack was drenched with sweat, and as Colonel Coleman was setting up the skirmish line Andy noticed that his brother had developed a crimson rash. "Go to the rear, Jack," he pleaded. "Find the field hospital. You're sick something terrible."

"Where's Oliver?" Jack inquired, kneeling down in the grass and leaning on his Enfield.

"Oliver's gone back to his regiment. He said last night you looked awful puny and ought to be in a doctor's care." Jack settled slowly over on his side and lay shaking in the weeds. Now the very worst occurred to Andy and he began to cry. Jack told him he shouldn't cry, but Andy said he couldn't help it, for he loved him.

"I'll see Howell," said Jack. He fainted away, and just then a double line of dismounted Yank cavalry came over a rise in front and advanced on them, hastened along by a little man on horseback wearing hip-boots and a hat with its brim looped up by a gold star. This man had blond mutton-chops and was waving a straight sword. At his command, the Yanks opened fire with their short carbines. The balls flew hissing past Andy where he bent anxiously over Jack. Captain Bristol ran up and asked if Jack were hit. "No, sir," Andy cried over the crackle of musketry as the 39th began to shoot back at the oncoming Yanks. "He's sick and needs nursing."

Artillery batteries on both sides had started up now, and the shells passed overhead, wailing like unhappy infants. Andy and Captain Bristol looked up and saw battalions of Yank infantry advancing in masses behind the cavalry skirmish line. "Leave him," the captain said. "Can't you see he's got the measles? He'll infect the whole damn regiment." He motioned towards the enemy with the snout of his revolver. "They can give him the care he needs. It's better he infects them than us anyhow."

Andy argued against it, weeping, but Captain Bristol would not relent. "We're withdrawing this skirmish line, Andy," he insisted. "That's Osterhaus and Smith of Logan's Fifteenth Corps coming yonder." Andy knelt and took up

Jack in his arms while the carbine bullets and Minie balls spouted dirt over them. Jack's body was limber and hot as a stove and his clothes were sodden with sweat. Andy called his name time and again till Captain Bristol ordered Johnny Deal and Danny Davis to come and drag him off. Jack lay alone in the hot grass dreaming.

Afterword

● ● ●

Joseph T. (Jack) Curtis, Private, Company E, 39th North Carolina Infantry, prisoner of war Number 548, died of measles on Monday the sixth of June, 1864, in the U.S. Army General Hospital at Nashville, Tennessee. He was buried in Plot Number 6252 of the Nashville City Cemetery. He was twenty-two years of age.

Andy Curtis and Oliver Price fought through the rest of the war in some of its worst battles and survived, though Oliver was shot in the right leg at the battle of Bentonville in Eastern North Carolina and walked on crutches from time to time all the rest of his life. Notwithstanding his wound, he did move to Clay County after the war to farm as he had planned.

Andy Curtis's youngest sister Rebecca, who kept a pet hen in an upstairs wardrobe during the war, grew up and married a man named Thomas Carter, and in 1883 they had a daughter named Lilly.

Oliver Price's son Syl grew up, married, and fathered a girl named Minnie and a boy named Will. When his wife died, Syl placed his children in the care of two brothers and their wives and vanished, never to be heard from again. These brothers whom I have called Jimmy and Andy Cartman, lived when they were children at Madison Curtis's place, pretending to be twins.

In 1902 Lilly Carter married Will Price. They had eight children. One of these, Edgar Price, was my father.

Hiwassee is a work of fiction, but it is based in part on the factual history of Western North Carolina and of my father's family. All of the persons in the Curtis and Price families mentioned in the book actually lived and were my forebears, though in a couple of instances I have thought it best to change names to respect the sensitivities of living descendants. The Civil War service records of Jack, Andy and Howell Curtis and Oliver Price were as I describe them. The names of their officers and messmates are taken from the actual muster rolls of the 39th and 65th North Carolina and the 39th Georgia regiments.

The tragic circumstances of the war in the mountains are accurately portrayed, although I have taken some liberties with the timing of events. Bridgeman, the Quillens and the Pucketts are fictitious, but regrettably had their real-life counterparts in Clay and Cherokee at the time. The Yellow Jacket raid is imaginary, but is consistent with the facts of real raids conducted in that region by a bushwhacker leader named George Kirk and by others.

Hiwassee could be described as a meditation on the conjectural history of a family. Events such as those in this book certainly happened to persons in Western North Carolina in the 1860's, and could even have happened to my ancestors, though I cannot prove that they did. In writing the book I meant to honor them. I hope I have.

—Charles F. Price
Cattail Creek, N.C.
January, 1996

Glossary

Beeves—plural of beef cows

Calash—a kind of buggy

Clabber—milk that has soured and curdled

Dirteaters—farmers, or a pejorative term for poor whites

Elephant—to have "seen the elephant" is to have been in battle

Jasper—fellow

Osnaburg—a heavy, coarse fabric in a plain weave

Outliers—deserters from either army

Po'-buckra—originally a slave term for whites which evolved into a pejorative term for poor white trash

Poke—bag or sack

Secesh—secessionist

Tackeys—poor whites

Tory—Union sympathizer